# GODDESS OF FLAMES

KINGDOM OF FAIRYTALES BOOK 4

J. A. ARMITAGE

Edited By Rose Lipscomb

Cover by Enchanted Quill Press

Proof Reader: Tina Merritt

❀ Created with Vellum

# KINGDOM OF FAIRYTALES

You all know the fairytales, the stories that always have the happy ending. But what happens after all those storybook characters get what they wanted? Is it really a happily ever after?

In this prequel, you will find out what happens next, be transported back to those lands you fell in love with and be prepared to meet some new characters along the way.

Kingdom of Fairytales is a new way of reading with one chapter a day and one book a week throughout the year beginning January 1st

**Lighting-fast reads you won't be able to put down**

Read in real time as each chapter follows a day in the life of a character throughout the entire year, with each bite-sized episode representing a week in the life of our hero.

Each character's story wrapped up at the end of every season with a brand new character and story featured in each season.

**Fantasy has never been so epic!**

# READING ORDER

Kingdom of Fairytales is a 52 book series split into thirteen seasons. Each season has a four book story arc of a fairytale character with the last season seeing them all coming together. You can read any series first with the exception of thirteen, however it is recommended that you read in the order below...

PREQUEL

SLEEPING BEAUTY

1. Queen of Dragons
2. Heiress of Embers
3. Throne of Fury
4. Goddess of Flames

LITTLE MERMAID

5. Queen of Mermaids
6. Heiress of the Sea
7. Throne of Change
8. Goddess of Water

RED RIDING HOOD

9. King of Wolves
10. Heir of the Curse
11. Throne of Night
12. God of Shifters

RAPUNZEL

13. King of Devotion
14. Heir of Thorns
15. Throne of Enchantment
16. God of Loyalty

RUMPELSTILTSKIN

17. Queen of Unicorns
18. Heiress of Gold
19. Throne of Sacrifice
20. Goddess of Loss

BEAUTY AND THE BEAST

21. King of Beasts
22. Heir of Beauty
23. Throne of Betrayal
24. God of Illusion

ALADDIN

25. Queen of the Sun
26. Heiress of Shadows
27. Throne of the Phoenix
28. Goddess of Fire

CINDERELLA

29. Queen of Song
30. Heiress of Melody
31. Throne of Symphony

32. Goddess of Harmony

ALICE IN WONDERLAND

33. Queen of Clockwork
34. Heiress of Delusion
35. Throne of Cards
36. Goddess of Hearts

WIZARD OF OZ

37. King of Traitors
38. Heir of Fugitives
39. Throne of Emeralds
40. God of Storms

SNOW WHITE

41. Queen of Reflections
42. Heiress of Mirrors
43. Throne of Wands
44. Goddess of Magic

PETER PAN

45. Queen of Skies
46. Heiress of Stars
47. Throne of Feathers
48. Goddess of Air

URBIS

49. Kingdom of Royalty
50. Kingdom of Power
51. Kingdom of Fairytales
52. Kingdom of Ever After

KINGDOM
OF
FAIRYTALES
URBIS PRISON
SHIPLEY
THE VALE
AZREN
BADALAH
KISBU
DESERT
DRACONIS
ZHORE
MOSA
ABORIA
ELDER
URBIS
AZURE
ENCHANTIA
EMERALD CITY
OZ
SKYLA
FLORIS
TULIS
THE FORGE
ARCADIA
RENAIS
MELTALL
ATLANTICE
ANTLA

## 22ND JANUARY

"What were you thinking?" My father asked as he paced back and forth at the bottom of my bed, his face knotted with worry and stress. Stress that once again, I'd caused, although I had good reason.

I'd woken up with a headache and having my father shouting at me for a good ten minutes straight before I'd even thought about coffee, was not doing much to help it. Pain throbbed in my temples and pounded my brain like a carriage rolling over a rocky road.

I blinked a few times waiting for my father to take a pause in his diatribe so I could explain myself. "I told you. Charlotte and Caspian think Mother is stuck in a dream world and can't get out. The only way to release her is to find Derillen or Morpheus. As I don't know where Derillen is, I was on my way to Urbis to track down Morpheus."

My father massaged his temples and stopped his pacing. "Yes, I heard what you said, but you were being carried by a dragon, Azia. A dragon! Haven't you seen the damage they've caused? No wonder Jacob shot you down. He thought you were being abducted. Now I know you have something weird going on with them, but I can't expect everyone to know that. Heck, I don't want anyone to know that. I've told you before to stay away from them. Whatever you think, they are wild creatures. I don't care that they are shifters. They are still animals."

"What about Nyre?" I asked. "Where is she?"

Six beds filled the castle hospital wing altogether. When occupied, green curtains separated them, but now, all the curtains were pulled back, showing me that I was the only patient in the room. Nyre wasn't in any of the beds.

"And what is this nonsense about Morpheus?" my father continued, ignoring my question. "I didn't bring you up to be religious. The gods are made up for people who don't know any better. As a princess, you shouldn't align yourself with any religion. We have to show impartiality in such matters. If we go to a place of worship for one religion, we'd have to go to all of them, and do you know how many gods there are? Hundreds, if not thousands. It seems that everyone has their own personal god these days."

I pulled myself up in the bed as he ranted. "Maybe we are the ones that don't know any better, Father... Where's Nyre?"

"And I don't know how many times I have to tell you that Derillen is dead. I sent my men out to look for spindles because I thought there may be a copycat, but that doesn't mean I believe she is still alive. I may not have seen her body all those years ago, but there is no other reason that the brambles had begun to lose their magic when I broke through to free your mother. If she was still alive, we'd know about it."

I gripped the edge of one of my pillows in frustration. My friend was hurt, and I didn't know where she was. "Father," I emphasized, raising my voice. "Where is Nyre?" She had fallen from the sky when I did. The fall had knocked me out when I hit the ground, but I remembered the flapping of her wings as she valiantly tried to keep us up in the air.

"Who is Nyre?" My father asked with agitation. He stopped pacing and looked at me with a quizzical expression. "The dragon? It flew off when you hit the ground."

She flew off. I sighed with relief. If she could fly away, it meant she wasn't too injured. My fear subsided a little, and the pain that had begun to build up in my chest eased off.

"Was she hurt?" I asked.

"Does it really matter?" My father snapped. "She was able to fly back up the mountain if that answers your question. Jacob tried to get her, but she flew away too quickly."

"Yes, it matters," I shouted at him, a little louder than my aching brain could handle. "It matters because she is my friend, and she was helping me out. She was helping you out too. You've said many times you'd do anything to help mother, and that's exactly what we were doing. No one else can help her. How many doctors have you paraded through here, and not one of them has been able to do so much as to make mother blink? At least, Nyre was willing to help, and she's never even met Mother!"

My father's tone softened a little, but I could still hear the hard edge to it. "I don't want to argue with you, Azia. You have a busy week coming up what with the competition. I need you back to health before that starts. Dr. Augusto looked you over last night, and he said that you have no broken bones. A few bruises, but he said you can get up on your feet whenever you like..." Dr. Augusto and a nurse were the two members of staff that worked in the small hospital wing in the castle. Dr Augusto was one of the first people to check on my mother when she first fell asleep, though he didn't know what was wrong with her any more than any of the so-called experts had.

I made to get out of bed, but my father stopped me.

"...Once you've rested. I want you to stay here this morning, and then after lunch if you feel better, you may get up. I have business to attend to."

He turned on his heels.

"What's happening with the dragons?" I shouted as he walked away, but he left the hospital wing, closing the door behind him and leaving the question unanswered.

I needed to go up the mountain to warn the dragons. I'd thought this was all over, but I didn't trust my father not to go back on his word. Not with the mood he was in. I stood up, the floor cold beneath my bare feet, but a wave of nausea hit me, and my head began to spin.

"What are you doing, silly?"

The nurse, a young woman named Amelia, ran over and helped me back into bed. "I've got strict instructions from your father not to let you leave until you are well enough. You've bruised your right arm and leg, and you've probably got a concussion too. Why not lie back, and I'll bring you some breakfast. What do you fancy?"

"Coffee," I mumbled, needing to clear the wool from my brain.

She nodded, giving me a brief smile and headed to the small room where she made coffee.

An image of Milo hit me with such force, I had to lie back down. I needed him. However much I hated to admit I needed anyone, I needed him right now. I ached for him to pull me into his arms and kiss the pain away.

"Amelia," I shouted, sending an echo through my mind. She popped her head around the door.

"Everything okay?"

I nodded carefully. Even the slightest of movements sent shockwaves of pain rattling round my head.

"Has anyone been to visit me? Before I woke up, I mean?"

"No," she replied. "I'm sorry. I don't know why that chap of yours hasn't been in. He surely must know you've been hurt. The whole castle knows what happened."

"It's ok," I lied, though I knew exactly why he'd not been to see me. I'd not seen him since he'd thrown the Draconian Sentinel at me with the photo of Caspian and I kissing.

"I'm sure he'll be in later," Amelia mused, minutes later after handing me a cup of coffee. "Your father mentioned that he'd told him. I expect he's held up, that's all."

"My father told Milo?" I couldn't imagine my father speaking to Milo unless he had to. I guess having his daughter almost killed constituted as having to. I took a sip of the coffee, and slowly my brain became less fuzzy.

Amelia gave me a strange look, and then her face brightened. "Here's that chap of yours now. I told you he'd be here soon." She gave me a slight nudge on the arm and a wink before scurrying off to leave me alone with Milo.

My heart leapt until I turned and saw Caspian walking through the door with a huge bunch of flowers. That was who Amelia was talking about when she said my chap. She'd been talking about Caspian, not Milo.

"You are a fool," Caspian said, throwing the flowers down on a bedside cabinet next to me.

"I'm fine, thanks," I threw back in a snarl.

"At least, you've not ruined that pretty face of yours. I'd hate to be standing next to someone resembling a troll on my wedding day."

I glared at him, fury filling my every pore. Not even the threat of me almost dying was enough to elicit any kind of empathy in the jerk. "Please find somewhere else to exist, dirtball. I'm not in the mood."

He grinned at me in the same way he always did, flicking up the corners of his gorgeous mouth lazily, making me want to kiss those delicious lips of his and punch him in them in equal measures.

"I love it when you are angry," he said, pulling up a chair. "You've got that gorgeous death stare down to a tee. It's a sexy look on you."

The infuriating part about his last statement was that it forced me into his trap. I either did what I wanted and glared even harder, or I had to soften my features. I folded my arms, keeping my face as impassive as possible.

"What do you want, Caspian?"

"Actually, I've come to update you on the competition, now that your attempts to run away from it were thwarted."

"I wasn't running from the competition," I spat out.

He cocked his head to one side and considered me. "Do you really take me for a fool?"

"Yes," I replied. "Most of the time, but you know I wasn't running from the competition. I was heading to Urbis to find Morpheus."

"So you say," Caspian said, "but you could have waited until after the competition. Until after our wedding."

"The wedding," I emphasized. "Not our wedding. How many times do I have to tell you I'm not marrying you?"

"Roughly the same amount of times I have to assure you that you are, I expect," he replied with a laugh. "I brought you some flowers. Aren't you going to thank me?"

He picked them up and handed them over. One of the flower heads fell from the stem onto the bed. It reminded me of the poppy Milo had given me a while back. The one that must have cost him a week's wages. These flowers probably cost a month's wages, but money was not something Caspian had to bother about, judging by his flashy clothes. Plus, he was living here rent-free. That must be worth a bunch of flowers or two. I pushed them away, and he put them back on the nightstand.

"Nope," I said.

"Hmm, well then," he sighed. "I'll just tell you about the competition and be on my way. Four judges have been appointed, and a stadium of sorts is being erected on the grounds. At final count, there are nine hundred and eighty-three men competing. The first round will whittle them down to a hundred, the second to ten, and then the last round will choose the winner...me."

I rolled my eyes. At least with so many men competing, the chances of him winning were slim. Slimmer than he thought.

"As I'm a competitor," he carried on, "I will stay in a tent behind the arena. From Friday, I, along with the other competitors, will sleep and eat in there. The judges will not allow me to talk to you during the competition."

"At least something good has come of all this then," I quipped. "I might get a break from you." The morning was shaping up better than I expected. Caspian only had a one in nearly one thousand chance of winning the competition, and I wouldn't have to speak to him for three days. Marvelous.

"Quite," he said lazily. "Your father has chosen the judges, and before you get all pissy, no, I didn't have a hand in choosing any of them. I don't even know them. The head judge is one of your father's guards. Jacob Hawkins."

"What?" I sat up straighter, and the headache that I'd managed to make subside thanks to the coffee now threatened to come back with a vengeance. "He's the man that shot me down. He's an asshole! He wants my father to go and kill all the dragons. Dragon balls, the man is more of a creep than you are."

"Never the less," Caspian continued, obviously not bothered about the dragons, or my derogatory term for him. Not that Caspian was ever bothered by anything that didn't affect him directly. "He's taken over the administration of the competition and made himself head judge. Your father signed off on it, so there is nothing you can do. The second is a member of staff at the local newspaper, Harry Parkes, third, some woman named Gina who is the headmistress at a local school, and fourth is some actor guy who I'm assured is famous here, though I've never heard of him. They were picked because of their backgrounds and impartiality, so don't get your panties in a bunch over it."

I sipped at my coffee and tried to keep my composure. I didn't care about the three other judges, but I hated Jacob with a passion.

"Have you seen Milo at all?" I asked, changing the subject. Asking Caspian about Milo was another thing I hated, but who else could I ask? Amelia didn't even know him.

Caspian sat back in his chair and folded his arms, a sly grin creeping over his face. "So he's not been to visit you then? Well, I didn't think much to the guy. Why have burger when you can have steak? That's what I say."

"Don't you have somewhere to be?" I asked, suddenly tired. "What about Charlotte? Why not go and bother her?"

"I've just seen her. We dined together. Why do you want me to see Charlotte?"

How was the man so utterly blind? "You know you keep telling me how you can read bodies, that you can understand body language? Well, how can you be so good at that and so confoundingly stupid at the same time? The girl is completely besotted with you. She'd walk to the ends of the kingdom on glass in bare feet if you asked her to."

"She has a little crush on me," he said, waving his hand airily.

"A little crush?" I huffed. "She spent every penny she had getting the Urbis Express here just because you asked her to. She didn't come to see the Draconis castle, and she certainly didn't come to see me."

"Pft! Nothing that will stop our wedding. You don't need to worry about her."

I opened my mouth to tell him he had a better chance of a skunk wanting to marry him than me when the door behind him opened.

"I'm sorry, I shouldn't have come." My heart almost exploded with joy as I saw Milo over Caspian's shoulder.

"You should have come," I said, pulling the covers off myself. "Caspian was just leaving. Isn't that right?" I gave Caspian a pointed look.

He ignored it and sat further back in his chair. "Actually Mikey, Azia and I were just talking about our wedding. It's shaping up to be a marvelous affair. Maybe you can be my best man...oh no, you can't. I'm the best man here."

Milo nodded and then closed the door behind him as he left the small ward.

"I really hate you, you know that?" I said, climbing out of bed and accidentally on purpose, spilling what was left of my coffee over his groin. It served him right. I only wished it was hotter.

I was dressed in only my nightgown, but that didn't stop me from chasing Milo down the corridor.

"Stop."

He stopped and turned. "I'm sorry for interrupting you. I guess you and your boyfriend were enjoying some quality time together."

"Don't do this," I begged, grateful that there was no one else in the corridor. I didn't need anyone else witnessing the painful exchange.

"Do what?" he asked. His face showed no emotion, but I could see in his eyes how difficult this was for him. He was hurting as much as I was.

"You know. Caspian isn't my boyfriend. You know he

only goads you to make himself feel important. What does that say about him?"

Milo sighed. "I don't know what that says about him, and I don't care. It doesn't matter. I only came to see if you were alright, and now that I can see you are, I'll be on my way."

"Please, don't," I whispered as he turned to walk away from me. I couldn't bear it. In a few days, I was going to be engaged, whether or not I liked it, and I wanted to spend my remaining time with Milo.

"You kissed him, Azia!" he shouted. "All this time, you've been telling me how much you despised the guy, and then you kissed him behind my back. How many times did it happen? Was it going on all that time we were together? I mean, you told me enough times that you didn't want to marry me. I guess I know why now, huh?"

"It wasn't like that," I said, tears streaming down my face. "He kissed me."

He breathed in deeply, his teeth gritted together. Only the slight tremble in his lip gave him away.

"I saw the photograph, Azia. The whole of Draconis saw it. Your eyes were closed. You were enjoying it."

I remembered the picture on the front cover of the Draconis Sentinel. He was right. I did appear to be blissfully happy with kissing Caspian. I was drunk. That was all. At least, that was the official line. The one I was sticking to.

"It doesn't matter anyway," he said. "I came in to say goodbye."

Suddenly, the kiss melted away into unimportance. "What do you mean goodbye? I thought you were going to enter the competition. You said you'd fight for me."

"I've nothing to fight for anymore. I've withdrawn my entry, and we both know that when you marry Caspian, I won't be needed in the castle anymore. He'll fire me the second your vows have been exchanged. I'm going before I get pushed."

"No one will push you!" I cried as he turned to walk away.

"You already have," he replied, leaving me alone in the corridor with only my tears.

## 23RD JANUARY

The noise of people talking outside my bedroom window woke me from a fitful sleep. I'd been warned that tents were being erected for the competition today and would it no doubt be noisy, but nothing had quite prepared me for how deafening it was. Dragging myself out of bed, I opened my curtains, surprised to find hundreds of men in the courtyard. On closer inspection, these were my father's guards and not people coming to erect tents. Beyond the castle walls, the people putting up the tents for the competition were there, so why were my father's men in the courtyard? Pulling on a dress, I headed outside to see what was going on.

My father was easy to spot in the center of the men. Although when I say spot, I heard him first rather than saw him, his voice booming out over the general throng

"What's happening, Father?" I asked, after pushing my way through the men. The man he was arguing with turned out to be Jacob. As soon as I saw him, a general feeling of unease settled in my stomach.

"We're going up the mountain!" Jacob replied for him. "We are going to kill the dragons before they kill you."

I was pretty sure my dying didn't bother him a jot, but he'd been desperate to take the army up to kill the dragons for a while, and now it looked like my father was going to give him a chance.

I turned to my father. "Why?" I argued. "I told you they wouldn't attack!"

He shot a glance at Jacob. "Look, Azia. This has been a long time coming. You've been seen twice in the grip of a dragon."

"You were lucky I managed to shoot you down last time," Jacob interrupted. "Who knows what would have happened to you if I hadn't?"

My anger spiked. "Lucky? You could have killed me. I spent the night in the hospital wing. You hurt Nyre."

"Who's Nyre?" Jacob asked, suspiciously.

"It's a friend of hers," my father said quickly. He obviously didn't want anyone to know that I'd voluntarily been flying with a dragon. It was much easier to pretend I was being kidnapped. "Azia, please go inside. This doesn't concern you. Thousands of people are coming to the competition, and I don't want any repeat performances from the dragons like they did before when they burned some of my men to death. I have the safety of the people to consider, not just yours."

"But..."

"Azia! Don't question me," he shouted sternly. "I've told you to go inside, and I expect you to do it."

Behind him, Jacob smiled smugly, and it took everything I had not to punch him.

I ran back into the castle, but I wasn't going to stay there. I'd made Vasuki a promise, and I intended to keep it. Once I was out of sight of my father, I dodged around the side of the castle and into the back garden, where I ran through the gate leading to the woods. At the other side of the woods, I shot a beam of light into the air.

This time, it wasn't Nyre that came to me, but Vasuki. His beautiful blue outstretched wings glided over me before he grabbed me in his talons and whisked me up the mountain. He dropped me in the same empty nest I'd come to when I first met him. This time there was only him there. He turned back into his almost human form.

"What is going on?" he snapped. "I thought that we had a deal. I did not expect Nyre to come home last night with an injury caused by your men."

I sucked in a breath, deciding how to handle it. He was usually so calm, but the way he looked at me left me in no doubt that his patience had worn a little too thin.

"You remember when I accused you of hurting the castle guard, and you told me it wasn't your doing? Well, those men hurting Nyre was none of my doing. How is she?"

He considered my words for a minute before replying. "The arrow caught her wingtip. It will heal, and she can still fly, but it hurt her." He emphasized the last words.

"I know it did," I said, clearing my throat. "I'm sorry. I didn't mean for any of this to happen. My father is being pushed into it by one of his men. The man has the backing of the people. Just like Darius with you, my father cannot control everyone."

Vasuki seemed to contemplate this. "I understand how difficult it is to run a kingdom. My kingdom is very small, just one colony, but I cannot sit back and let my people get hurt. I can't let my daughter get hurt."

"I understand," I said, wondering how he was going to take what I was about to say. "That's why I'm here. My father has ordered many of his men to come up the mountain. They are in the castle courtyard preparing for battle. You need to get all your dragons down into your village where the men cannot reach you."

Vasuki gave me a bitter smile then looked down to his feet. My chest felt weighed down as I awaited his response.

"I'm afraid we have moved beyond that," he said quietly before looking back up. "I cannot hide anymore. I've done what I can, but nothing will stop this. Now we have to fight, or they will keep on coming."

Fear gripped me. "No. Please don't. My brothers are in the army. They have to do what my father says. They are only fifteen and sixteen. I can't lose them, Vasuki. I've already lost my mother to a terrible curse."

"Nyre is only sixteen. They hurt her."

I nodded my head. "They did. I hate that they did, but they did. The man that shot her is the same man who is making my father send the army up here. He wants to kill you all, but my father doesn't. Not really. Jacob is putting him in an impossible situation."

"But your father is in charge," Vasuki pointed out. "He is the king, is he not? Who is this man who thinks he is above the king?"

I shook my head. Jacob was a nobody. "Before a few weeks ago, he was just one of my father's men. My father ordered him to build a wall at the base of the mountain to stop people coming up here. Jacob made it clear that he didn't like it. While my father was trying to find doctors and deal with a stupid competition, Jacob managed to persuade many people that you all need to die. My father's hands are tied. He doesn't want to hurt you. He knows you are shifters, but he has thousands of people coming for this competition, and he's been brainwashed into thinking that the dragons will hurt everyone."

"Then tell him we won't. I have no desire to send my dragons down the mountain to disrupt your human events."

I sighed. "I know that, but my father will no longer listen to me. When Nyre was seen carrying me, Jacob told everyone that I was being abducted. Now, more people are listening to him than my father, and my father is trying to do too much. He's not slept properly in weeks, and his own health is fading. Why can't you just send all your dragons to your village for a few days until this all blows over? It's not accessible by foot. You'll all be safe, and the worst that will happen to my father's men is that they will spend a day getting cold on the top of the mountain. They'll soon stop listening to Jacob after that."

Vasuki brought his hand to his mouth and chewed on his thumbnail. He paced around me, deep in thought.

"I cannot think of a way around this, Azia," he said. "I've told you that your magic draws us to you, and every fiber in my being wants to do what you say. I'm almost compelled to do your bidding, the magic is that strong, but I cannot take all the dragons down to the village. Dragon eggs are laid in nests like this one for a reason. The baby dragons need the high altitude to grow and to hatch. If we take the eggs down, many will not hatch. I cannot ask the mothers to leave their eggs, and I cannot ask them to bring them down to the village. In hiding, my people will be killed just the same as if we fight. I have no desire to fight, but I do not have a choice. Please don't force me to leave them."

Don't force him to. I knew my bond with them was strong, but I didn't understand how much until now. I could make them flee, but then the deaths of their babies would be all on me.

He pleaded with me with his eyes. This wasn't the same strong Vasuki I knew. This was a man in an impossible position...just like my father.

"I've made so many mistakes in the past few weeks," I said, thinking of Milo and the competition, which was ultimately the reason my father was sending his men up in the first place. "I'm not about to make another. I will not force you to move the eggs, and I will not force you to not fight."

The relief on his face was obvious. He breathed out a sigh.

"I cannot let you fight alone, though. Take me back down the mountain, please."

He regarded me suspiciously. "Why? What are you going to do?"

"I'm going to get dressed in something better than this," I said, indicating my dress. "It's freezing up here."

Vasuki transformed back into the magnificent beast he was, and this time, waited for me to climb up onto his back before he flew me down the mountain. In the distance, my father's men were already beginning the climb. After dropping me at the bottom, Vasuki opened his wings once more and took off into the sky, presumably, to round up the other dragons. I couldn't use my magic to stop him fighting now that I knew what was at stake, but there was a lot at stake on my side too. My father was going up there and no doubt Hollis and Ash too. At least Milo had left us. It was the only consolation in him leaving. I wouldn't have to worry about him being blasted by dragon fire.

I raced back into the castle and up to my room. Jack stood guard alone on the corridor. My heart skipped when I thought of how weird it was that Milo wasn't there helping, but I had more urgent things to deal with to be mooching over a broken heart. In my room, I pulled on some warm trousers and a tunic, which I covered in the leather armor that Milo had brought for me back when we'd both started practicing swordsmanship. Picking up the dragon sword, I raced back out of the room as quickly as I could so Jack wouldn't have time to stop me. The castle bustled with people caught up in last-minute problems associated with the competition. No one paid me any mind as I dashed through, my sword by my side.

I had no idea how the men had managed to get over the wall, but I needed help to get over it. A pair of ladders that had been left behind in the fall were still in the garden, so I took them and managed to get over the wall that way.

The men had a huge head start on me, but I'd climbed this mountain before, and I had something they didn't. I had the lives of the dragons to save. I didn't know how I could stop this. I was winging it in the worst possible way, but I couldn't sit in my room watching people I loved go out to fight with other people I loved. I knew I needed to be there, I just didn't know what to do when I got there.

To my left, I could just about see the men in the distance. Their guard uniforms stood out against the white snow and gray stone. Once we were further up, the redness of the rock would camouflage them. I planned to be ahead of them by that point.

My lungs burned, and my muscles ached with the effort of climbing the mountain, but thoughts of what would happen if I didn't spurred me on. My half-assed idea was to wait until my father got to the top and position myself between him and his men, and the dragons. Would it stop either side? I didn't know. My father wouldn't attack if he knew I would get hurt, but Jacob would fell me himself if it meant killing dragons.

Minutes turned into hours and exhaustion began to kick in, but a quick glance to my left told me I was in the lead. Pushing past the fatigue was hard, but I was so close to the top, I could see it. The dragons were already there, lined up along the craggy top. All of them perched along the mountain, waiting for the onslaught. None of them took to the skies, but as I moved closer, I could see Darius itching to be off. If only I could pit Darius against Jacob and leave the pair of them to it, then I'd be fine. Unfortunately for everyone else involved, I had no say in the matter.

The snow-covered rocks made climbing hard as I edged around the mountain. One by one, the dragons glanced my way before settling their eyes back on my father's army of men.

At the very front, my father led the group, closely followed by Jacob, who was the only one of the men to hold his sword out, ready for attack. When they were within about fifty feet of the dragons, my father came to a stop and held his hand to the side to stop Jacob or any of the others from running past him.

I could see, even from the distance between us, the indecision in his eyes. He didn't want to do this anymore than I wanted him to. He was doing it because, in the past few weeks, the kingdom had fallen through the cracks, and though he knew they wanted a strong leader, he was not able to be one. The man had barely slept, and I'd not seen him at any meals for days. It was a miracle he was still standing, let alone able to climb a mountain leading a hundred men into battle. He was doing it because this was what people like Jacob needed to see. But in doing so, it meant Jacob got his way, and Jacob's way meant the destruction of a whole colony of Dragon shifters. I don't know what he had against dragons. He had no family hurt when the dragons came down the mountain and killed some of my father's men. Perhaps some of his friends had died, and he wanted retaliation. Maybe he wanted to steal dragon eggs to make some money. Maybe he just wanted to fight for the sake of it because that's what people like Jacob liked to do. I didn't know. I saw what was about to happen with absolute clarity. Both sides lined up ready to attack. The men with their swords, the dragons with their hot fiery breath. Not even running between them would stop them. Not with the likes of Jacob involved. But then, I knew what I had to do. Vasuki had told me that I could command him with my magic. I could compel him to do anything like some sort of dragon tamer, and if I pushed my magic hard enough, he would have to do it whether or not he liked it. I didn't want to force him to do anything, and I hoped it wouldn't come to it as I reached out to him with my magic. Before, I'd been throwing it out willy-nilly, and the dragons had come to me, urged on by the bright lights my magic produced. This time, I concentrated my magic on Vasuki alone. He cocked his head to one side and looked at me questioningly. He understood what I wanted without me telling him. This wasn't telepathy. I wasn't speaking to him in my mind. It was almost as though I was a part of him, and he was a part of me. I'd finally gotten my magic to work the way it was supposed to. I nodded my head at him, giving the explicit yes he needed. He crouched lower then pushed hard, unfurling his magnificent wings and taking to the sky. The men watched as he circled then fell into a dive. My father didn't have a chance. He'd not even had the time to pull his sword from his sheath.

Vasuki had him gripped between his teeth rather than in his claws. I winced at the thought of how uncomfortable it must have been, and how sooty Vasuki's breath was, but my father was wearing leather armor and would survive. If I played this right, everyone would. Vasuki turned mid-air and dived for me. He whisked us both to a nest away from my father's men. Behind him, another dragon sat. This one was bright yellow with orange-tipped wings. Vasuki shifted into his human form.

My father knew he was a shifter, but it didn't stop the look of astonishment on his face when Vasuki held his hand out for my father to shake.

My father stood still, his hands firmly by his side, wary of the shifter before him.

"This is Vasuki, Father," I explained." He is the king of the dragons. You would never listen to me when I told you that they don't want to fight, but maybe you'll listen to him."

"The dragon behind me is Kuda," Vasuki said, indicating the dragon. It watched us with frightened eyes. "Kuda was very young, sitting on her first batch of eggs eighteen years ago when some men stole into her nest. Not only did they steal her eggs, they also killed the hatchlings. Her babies would be the same age as Azia now, give or take a few months. Kuda never dared lay eggs after that. The thought of men coming and killing her babies stopped her. This year, she finally found the courage to lay again. You can't see them, but under her are five dragon eggs. They may be priceless artifacts to you, but to a grieving mother, they are her whole life. Kuda isn't the only dragon nesting. There are more. I do not want to hurt you or your men. I never did, but you understand that I will do what I have to do to keep them safe."

My father stood stock still; indecision plastered all over his face. I felt sorry for him. There was no winning here. He wasn't a bad person, and he could no more take those eggs from Kuda than I could.

"You don't understand." He turned to me. "Azia, you don't know what's been going on. Jacob has been organizing an uprising. If I don't let him fight the dragons, he will bring an army of his own to help him. Why do you think he is on the panel of judges at your competition? I ignored what was happening for so long because I was worried about your mother, about you." He turned back to Vasuki again. "I want no bloodshed. My sons are down there as are men that are far braver than me. They are waiting for my order to attack. If I don't give it, Jacob will."

"Then I can't help you. I will fly you back down to your men. When you give the order, they will attack us. At that point, I cannot stop my dragons from defending themselves. You might have swords, but we have the advantage of fire and height. You cannot win this."

"I know," my father said despondently. "I'm sorry it has come to this. I tried. I really did. I built a wall."

"No!" I screamed. "Father, you are signing a death wish. What about Ash and Hollis. What about me?"

"Ash and Hollis knew what they were doing when they came up the mountain. You can stay here. You will be safe. Maybe Kuda and her eggs will be safe too."

"You can't do this!" I screamed. I'd lost my mother, I was about to lose my brothers, and I'd lost the man I looked up to. The man I respected.

I ran towards him, but I was too late. Vasuki had transformed quickly and grabbed him in his talons, leaving me in a nest, too high up to do anything other than watch on in terror from above.

I sat on the very edge of the nest. Another two inches more, and I would plummet to my death. Vasuki had chosen this nest on purpose. He didn't want me in the line of fire any more than my father did. They both knew I'd run between them and, in doing so, would get myself killed.

Vasuki dropped my father to the ground about twenty feet above my father's army and thirty feet or so below the line of dragons. No one had made a move yet, both sides waiting for their leader to come back.

I could stop this. I could use my magic and compel the dragons to retreat, but in doing so, I was leaving their eggs vulnerable. Kuda's eggs would be safe, no matter what Vasuki said. The sheer cliffs around her nest protected her, but there were so many dragons that weren't—the mother dragons who had roosted on lower outcrops and nests.

Vasuki would never forgive me. I would never forgive myself, but then would I be able to forgive myself if I let my father and brothers perish in dragon fire? The thought of it burned at my heart.

"I'm sorry," I whispered as I began to pull my magic in. Pulling the dragons back would mean the baby dragons would die. The hatchlings, the eggs, but by not pulling them back, everyone would die.

A hand on my shoulder ripped away my concentration, and my magic ceased. I turned to find Kuda in her near-human form. Her bright yellow hair was greying at the temples, and laughter lines gave away her age.

"Don't do it," she said. It wasn't a warning. She spoke with a soft voice. "Your father still has time."

I turned to look back over the edge. She was wrong. There was no time. Both sides were ready to fight. One word from my father and chaos would happen.

He held his hand up in the air at around the same time that Kuda gripped mine. She dangled her feet over the edge and sat next to me.

I held my breath, almost unable to watch the inevitable onslaught.

"I..." my father began but faltered. I could just about hear him even at the distance separating us.

He walked forward, climbing the incline towards the dragons. No one else moved.

"What is he doing?" I whispered. "He's going to get himself killed."

"He did sound like a man on the edge," Kuda said, taking my hand in hers. "Maybe he thinks this is his only way out."

So that was my father's plan. Suicide by dragon so he didn't have to deal with any repercussions about what he was about to do.

Just as I thought things couldn't get any worse, he pulled his sword from his sheath and charged at Vasuki. With just one strike, Vasuki crashed to the floor. I screamed as my father brought his sword down, again and again, raining blows upon Vasuki's body. Nobody else moved. The dragons and the humans watched on. Jacob yelled something in excitement, but I didn't hear it over my own scream.

"He is dead!" My father shouted. "The king of the dragons is no more."

Below him, the men cheered, but the dragons didn't attack. They took to the skies, flying away quickly.

"Without their king, they are cowards," Jacob roared, charging to my father to bring him into a hug. "We are the victors."

Tears streamed down my face as I took in the scene below. My brothers were safe, but Vasuki was dead.

"They will not attack again," My father shouted. "Tonight, we go back down the mountain and celebrate our victory."

The men cheered again, relieved in the fact that none of them had been broiled alive. Only Jacob didn't move.

"Now hang on," he huffed." You killed one dragon. What about the others?"

"I killed the king of dragons," my father countered. "You saw how quickly the others fled. They will not dare to come down and fight anymore. Not without their leader. Come and have a drink with me as a guest in the castle."

Bile filled my throat as I thought of the pair of them drinking over Vasuki's death.

"What about the eggs?" Jacob asked.

My father shook his head. "They are eggs. They will die without the warmth of their mothers. We do not need to worry about them now."

"But...but. They are worth a lot of money."

My father put his arm over Jacob's shoulder and began to lead him down the mountain. "Come now, Jacob, you wouldn't want the people to think we were only coming up here to steal eggs. Not a man in such a high position as yourself. We have nothing to worry about now. Let's leave it at that."

Jacob didn't look too happy, but there was nothing he could do.

I watched them walk down the mountain until they were mere dots.

"You are shivering lass," Kuda said. "I'd take you back down the mountain, but as your father himself said, my eggs will die if I leave them too long without warmth. I expect Vasuki will do it for you."

"Vasuki?" I murmured. "Vasuki is dead."

"Am I?"

I nearly fell over the side of the nest as Vasuki spoke. I turned quickly to find him in his human form next to me.

"I saw my father kill you!" I whispered. my heart beating a percussion in my chest.

Vasuki smiled. "You saw your father hitting a stone between my wing and my body. I'm glad to know I am such a good actor that I fooled you as well as your father's army. I really expected more from you.You are my queen, after all. If one of the dragons really died, you would feel it."

"But how?"

They hadn't planned this. There was no time when just the two of them were together in the nest.

Vasuki gave me a smile. "It was your father's idea. He told it to me as I flew him back to his army. I couldn't answer, of course, so he had to hope I'd heard and would play along. Did I really do that good a job of dying?"

"Er, yeah," I nodded. "What about the other dragons? Why didn't they attack?"

"You are not the only one who can compel the dragons. You might be the queen of dragons, but I am the king." He gave me a wink. "Please tell your father I'd like to see him when he is ready. We might have tricked this Jacob character for now, but I doubt he will let this rest. I'd like to see if we can figure out a peaceful solution to all this."

I nodded my head, amazed at what had just transpired. My father was the leader I knew him to be, after all. He just needed to be put in a position where he could show his true colors. He needed a push. I laughed as Vasuki transformed and flew me back down to the woods.

# 24TH JANUARY

My father woke me up the next morning by knocking on my door.

"I came to apologize for not doing better," he said, shutting the door behind him so Jack couldn't eavesdrop. "I should have stood up to Jacob, but I was afraid of the repercussions. It was wrong of me."

I jumped out of bed and flung myself into his arms. "Are you kidding? You were amazing. No one was hurt."

"What about Vasuki? I assume it was he who flew you home."

"Yes. He'd like to speak to you," I replied. "He wants peace, and he'd like to make sure that nothing like yesterday ever happens again."

My father nodded and sat on the bed. "I want that too. I will go up and speak with him once the competition is over. I managed to get Jacob drunk last night, and he's forgotten about the eggs, but I'm sure once the competition is done with, he'll find a way to go back up. It's very clear that's all he's interested in. The danger of the fight and the monetary gain if he steals the eggs."

"Why not throw him off the judging panel?" I asked. I didn't like the thought of that man helping decide my own fate.

My father shrugged his shoulders." He was the one who instilled himself as a judge, but I think it's the best place he can be right now. It's keeping him occupied, and if he's busy with the competition, he won't have time to go back up the mountain. Besides, I saw your competition ideas. How much trouble can he cause when all he has to do is oversee the question of who is the queen of dragons?"

"You know who that is, right?" I grinned at him.

"I have my suspicions." He brought me into a hug. It was the first genuine father-daughter moment we'd had together in weeks, and I didn't want to let it go. "You know, when I saw your beautiful face for the first time, I never in my wildest dreams understood how amazing you'd turn out to be, nor all the gray hairs I'd get just watching you have your adventures. You were the type of child that would scrape her knee and then get right back up without flinching. I will never understand how you came to be the queen of the dragons, but I can't say that it surprises me."

Later on, once Father had left, Dahlia came to my room to wake me up and bring me coffee. In all the years I'd known her, she'd never brought me breakfast in bed. Not that a cup of coffee could be construed as breakfast, but it was close.

"I heard on the grapevine that Milo is leaving," she said warily, placing the coffee on my nightstand.

The adventure yesterday had kept my mind away from the heartbreak, but now that she'd mentioned his name, the pain came back full force.

"I know," I replied, trying to keep my emotions out of my voice. "He was worried that Caspian would fire him."

Dahlia shook her head "Why would he worry about a

thing like that? Caspian has no say in what goes on in this castle, no matter how much he likes to think he does. He could no more fire Milo than I could. Anyway, that's not what I mean. He came to the admin office this morning and asked for a reference. He says he's leaving Zhore."

I sat bolt upright in bed. "Leaving Zhore? Where is he going?"

Dahlia shrugged. "I don't know, Maureen, the head of admin didn't tell me, but she did get the feeling it wasn't only Zhore he was leaving. She thinks he might be leaving Draconis altogether."

Pulling back the covers, I jumped out of bed and ran to the door.

"Where do you think you're going?" Dahlia asked, rushing over to me and holding her hand to the door so I couldn't open it.

"Please, let me out," I cried, trying to get past her. "I need to find Milo before he leaves the castle."

"He already left the castle," Dahlia pointed out.

I shook in frustration. "Then I'll go to his house."

Dahlia looked me up and down. "In your pajamas?"

Damn! I pulled on some jeans and a t-shirt, and this time, Dahlia let me leave. I ran all the way to Zhore, muddying up the bottoms of my trousers in the process on the snow that was quickly melting and mixing with thawed mud underneath. The streets of Zhore were quiet, but the beginnings of the decorations for the wedding had already been erected in the main square. Even though my wedding was to take place in the castle, the people wanted to celebrate themselves. In the dim morning light and with the hint of fog that was drawing in, the whole thing looked as miserable as my own heart. I knocked loudly on Milo's door, willing it to open, but he wasn't in.

"Please, don't have already gone!" I whispered to myself. I

couldn't bear it. The pain of him leaving without saying goodbye was indescribable, but no one answered, so I had to conclude he had already left. I began the walk home, pain filling my chest, and as I passed the Dragon Roost Inn, I decided to go in on the off chance he was having a very early morning drink.

The bar was as dim as it had been the first time I'd gone in, the day I'd told Milo about our fake relationship. Just thinking about it pierced my chest. The place was almost empty save for the barmaid, Lisa, and a couple of other customers.

"A beer please," I said, scrabbling in my pocket for some loose change. She slammed down a beer in front of me, sloshing it all over the counter, as I realized I'd come out without any money.

"I'm afraid I don't have any cash on me." I apologized, trying to explain. "I'll bring some down next time I come."

She pulled the beer out of my reach and moved her face closer to mine. "Then, I'll pour you more beer the next time you come."

Yeah, this girl might not have recognized me as the princess, but she sure as shit knew I was the girl Milo came in here with.

I almost apologized to her for existing when someone sidled up beside me and tapped my shoulder.

"I'll pay for it," the person said, throwing down a couple of coins. Lisa begrudgingly pushed the beer back to me, slashing more on the counter for good measure. I turned to find Gladys standing next to me. The last time I'd seen her, she'd been at Milo's house. I was beginning to get used to her sneaking up on me.

"Shall we get a booth?" she asked, nodding at my beer. I picked the glass up and followed her to one of the darker booths.

"You won't find him," she said before I even had a chance to speak. "He's a good lad, that one, but his heart is broken."

"I know," I said. "I'm the one who broke it."

"I think that goes without saying, Lovie. I did tell him not to go getting mixed up with a princess, but would he listen? I told him that you were better suited to that fae chap in the paper. He's a man of power by the looks of his photo, and you, well, I already told you that you have power. Milo was just a normal lad, and normal never mixes well with power and money. You and he were like oil and water."

"I was more like Milo than you think," I replied, thinking of all the snatched moments in the castle, and all the times we practiced sword fighting out in the woods. Maybe I was raised a princess, but inside I was a warrior, a protector, just like Milo. Or at least I wanted to be.

Gladys called me out. She waggled her finger in my face. "Just because you like someone doesn't mean you are like them, and just because you dislike someone doesn't mean that you aren't the same. Take this fae fellow. Milo said he was an arrogant trumped-up ass, but he also said he was strong and resourceful, and eager to show people that he was a capable leader. Now doesn't that sound like you?"

"Not really? I'm no leader." And I didn't want to think of myself as being like Caspian.

She raised her eyebrows. "That's not the impression I get from reading the papers. I don't see your father doing much these days, but you are in the paper every day, giving interviews, reassuring the people. I saw what you said about your future husband, that he'll never be king and never be above you. You are stronger than you think you are."

I sighed. "I don't feel very strong at the moment," I said, nursing my beer. I was yet to take a sip of it.

"That's your heart talking. Ignore it for a moment and listen to your brain. What do you want?"

"At the moment, I want Milo."

"No," she said, smiling kindly. "Look beyond Milo. What do you want for you? And don't tell me you want to save your mother and you want to not have to do this competition thing you've gotten yourself into. All of that is just circumstance you've found yourself in. What do you want for yourself?"

I thought about it. So many things had required my attention over the last few weeks, that I'd almost forgotten what it felt like to just be me. Three weeks ago, I'd just celebrated my eighteenth birthday. I remember wishing I had a horse. It seemed so silly now. "I want to run Draconis," I said firmly. "I want to be a good and fearless leader, and I want to be able to do it for myself, not with a husband because I've been told I have to. I don't want to be protected, I want to be the protector."

"Spoken like a true leader," she said, sitting back, a wide smile on her face. "Now, drink up that beer. I'd hate to see it go to waste."

I downed the beer, more because I was feeling sorry for myself than to feel less guilt that she had bought it for me. After her telling me not to think about Milo, my next question almost embarrassed me, but I had to find him.

"Do you know where Milo is?"

She shook her head. "That I cannot say. I've not seen much of him around here lately, but he is exactly where he is supposed to be. I feel it. You, on the other hand, are not. Why don't you go home and concentrate on doing what you need to do and leave Milo to nurse his wounds? If you are meant to see him again, you will."

I thanked her for the beer and left the pub after saying goodbye.

Back at the castle, I had nothing to do. Part of me wanted

to go to my room and lock the door. A couple of weeks ago, I would have done that and spent the afternoon crying over Milo. I couldn't be that girl anymore. I'd told Gladys that I was going to be a fearless leader, and fearless leaders didn't sob in bedrooms over guys. To take my mind off Milo, I decided to go to the castle administration office, which had now been taken over as the center of operations for the competition.

The admin staff, which usually consisted of a lady called Maureen, her two assistants, and her cat, had grown to a team of twelve over the past week, and still, they were swamped with paperwork.

Stacks of it piled up high filled the room, and as I closed the door behind me, a stack almost toppled, saved at the last second by a harassed-looking assistant.

"Final count is just over a thousand men," Maureen said when I found her at her desk hiding behind a pile of paper. Her cat snoozed on another pile of what looked to be applications of entry. A thousand men! That was even higher than the figure Caspian had given me days prior.

"How are the details for the competition going?" I asked, figuring out I should at least have half a clue of what was going on. The castle was filled with people, and everyone seemed to know what was going on except me.

Maureen brought her hand up to her necklace and twisted it around her fingers. "There's been a setback or two," she admitted. "We've ordered tons of clay for the first round, but the supplier dumped it outside without letting us know, and it dried out. I've put in another order, but it will be touch and go if it gets here on time."

"It was a stupid idea anyway!" someone piped up from the back of the room. I looked over the frantic workers' heads to see Jacob sitting with his feet up, smoking a cigar. Plumes of smoke wafted up to the ceiling.

"What are you doing here?" I snapped, deliberately not keeping the annoyance out of my voice.

"I'm helping is what I'm doing," he said. "This competition of yours has turned into a shit show, and someone has to run it."

"Maureen was running it perfectly fine," I said. "And please put the cigar out. It stinks."

"The only thing that stinks," he said, standing up and walking over, "is the organization of this competition. Who orders a ton of clay and then gets it delivered before the event starts?"

"Look, just do whatever you want!" I huffed. "Just get out of my sight."

He gave Maureen and me a filthy look and stubbed his cigar out on a stack of paperwork before heading out the door.

"I'm sorry about him," Maureen apologized, picking up the cigar and stack of paper, which thankfully hadn't been set alight. She tipped the lot in the garbage.

"The tents have been going up all week," Maureen enthused, changing the subject. "We have a temporary stadium, a huge tent for the competitors to sleep and eat in, and another to get changed in. I've ordered costumes for all of the competitors, and the entertainment is booked, so it's not all doom and gloom."

"Entertainment?" I inquired.

"Yes," she said, ticking something from a sheet on her clipboard." We have thousands of people coming to watch, so I've had to organize entertainment for before each part of the competition. This thing will go on for three days, and I don't want anyone getting bored. I've also got the kitchen working triple time and organized caterers from Zhore to help with the rest."

Clay problems aside, she seemed to have the whole thing

mostly in hand, and there was nothing I could do to help. This had started as my idea, and somewhere along the line, it had gotten out of control and run away without me. I'd started all of this as a way to get out of marrying Caspian and being able to marry Milo. He was right when I told him I wasn't ready for marriage. I'd told him over and over, not realizing how difficult it would be to hear. I had pushed him away.

"Do you have a list of all the contestants?" I asked Maureen.

A look of pure panic crossed her face before one of the other staff members passed a list to her.

"Oh, yes. I knew I had one somewhere. Here."

She passed it to me. The names were listed alphabetically by surname, although I noticed Caspian's name at the very top despite his last name being Montblanc. No doubt, he'd had a hand in it. I scanned down until I hit the k's. Milo's name was there, but with a thick black line through it. I'd hoped he would change his mind, but it was wishful thinking on my part. He'd gone. I'd lost him for good.

"Thank you, Maureen," I said despondently, passing her back the list.

"Don't you have a photoshoot later? "Maureen asked. "Maybe you should go and get ready for that."

"Do I?" I couldn't keep up with everything these days. There was so much going on, and what with dragons, competitions, and doctors, things like photoshoots were very low on my list of things to worry about. Still, just because I wasn't worried, didn't mean that Dahlia wouldn't be. I could imagine her running around the castle in an increasing state of panic looking for me.

"I should go," I sighed.

I found Dahlia in the state of panic I expected in the castle kitchens. She fit right in with the general air of stress in there. Food covered every surface, and the head chef barked orders at anyone who dared to come close to him.

"I thought you'd be down here trying to grab a sandwich, seeing as you missed breakfast," Dahlia said. "I managed to get you one. Here." She passed me a sandwich and bustled me out of the door. "They are making food for all the contestants, not to mention all the guests. The head chef has brought in a catering company to help, but now, they are taking over the kitchen, and he's not happy about it."

"What's the photoshoot for?" I asked, not really caring. "The Sentinel? Haven't they got enough photos."

"There can never be enough photos of you, but no. Reporters from all the kingdom's main newspapers have come in. We need you looking pretty."

"Great!" I replied sarcastically. I expected a complete shit show. After all, the whole thing had been a disaster from start to finish, but when I walked into the main hall, dressed up to the nines with my hair styled and my makeup on point thanks to Dahlia, the photographers were seated in chairs in a perfectly civilized manner, waiting for my arrival.

My father introduced me as I walked in. It was such a difference from the week before when a thousand men had been invited to meet me. I could hear a pin drop as I walked across the floor to a small stage that had been erected with a painted backdrop for the photos.

The reporters clapped politely as I took my father's hand and stepped up onto the stage.

"You look beautiful," he whispered as he took his place next to me. "Your mother would be proud."

I gave him a shy smile. It was nice having my father back to his usual self.

Photographers from the Sentinel, the Atlantice Conch, the Floris Observer, the Badalah Beacon, and all the others stood up to take photos of my father and me as we posed.

The prideful father and the almost-wedded daughter. The only kingdom not represented was Elder, which never seemed to care about what was going on in the other kingdoms. They didn't even have a newspaper as far as I was aware.

Once they'd finished photographing me posing with my father, who had also dressed up for the occasion, they wanted snaps of me on my own. I was painfully aware that my mother should have been standing by my side, but she was still upstairs wasting away in her bed.

After the photos, I readied myself for the onslaught of questions, but instead of the men and women reporters fighting over themselves, someone handed me a list and told me to choose which questions I wanted to answer. As far as photoshoots and press conferences went, it was one of the most pleasant I'd had to deal with.

"I told your father to warn them all to be civil," Dahlia confessed afterward as she took me back to my mother's dressing room. She would have had me dressed up in the beautiful dress all day, but she knew she'd have to listen to me complain about it. I pulled the dress off and stepped back into the jeans and t-shirt combo I'd left there before Dahlia went to work on removing my makeup. I hated wearing the stuff. It made my face itch.

She was taking the hairpins out when we both heard a crash next door. The room next to the dressing room was my parents' bedroom. I caught Dahlia's eyes in the mirror. My father was still downstairs talking to the reporters. There should be no one in my mother's room.

"Mother!" I shot up, almost knocking Dahlia over in the process. We both rushed to the room. My heart beat in triple time at the thought of my mother wakening up. She'd been asleep for so long. There was no other reason for the crash. Even if she'd fallen out of bed, it meant that she'd woken enough to move. I knew for a fact that the maid was not on duty at the moment.

Excitement filled me as we crashed through her door, but it was to be short-lived. She was still asleep in the same position we had left her in. Beside her, a photographer I recognized from the press conference was snapping away so intently he'd not even noticed when we came through the door. The crash we'd heard was a vase he'd knocked over which lay on the floor as water from it seeped into the carpet.

"What the hell are you doing?" Dahlia shouted, which made him finally take notice. Panic overcame his features as he tried to make a dash past us. I jumped in his way, blocking his path and grabbed his camera. There was no way in this kingdom. I was going to let him go with those pictures.

He was stronger than I anticipated, and the harder I pulled on the camera, the harder he pulled back. Beside me, Dahlia screamed and waved her hands around. The guy pushed me into the doorframe in an attempt to hurt me enough so I'd let go of the camera. My head smashed against the frame sending shockwaves through my body and causing me almost to black out. I cried out in pain as everything began to spin, but my grip on his camera only tightened. My mother had always prided herself on her appearance, and although she was as beautiful in sleep as she was awake, she would hate having those photos printed. And they wouldn't just be printed in the kingdom that this reporter creep was from. They would spread so that everyone would see them.

My head hit the frame again, and I felt the camera being tugged from my grasp. I wanted to hold on, but a surge of nausea overcame me.

I pulled in a deep breath to orient myself, but as my vision cleared, the reporter went flying past me, almost hitting me as he crashed into the wall next to me. Caspian ran towards him and punched him in the face, knocking him out cold. He waved his hand, and the camera gave a little sputter then erupted into a ball of flames that died as soon as they had appeared. What was left of the camera, Caspian threw at the unconscious reporter.

"Dahlia, please get a couple of guards to come and collect this garbage," Caspian said. "You'd better find out which kingdom he came from and get him on the first Airship home."

Dahlia nodded and ran off down the corridor.

I brought my hand to my head. Already a lump was forming somewhere under the hair and hairclips.

"Are you alright?" Caspian asked, bringing his hand up to my face. I'd never felt so vulnerable in his presence before. I nodded. I would be alright, but it had shocked me. What with everything else going on, I'd not thought I'd need to worry about protecting my mother from photographers.

"I'm sorry you had to deal with that," he said, caressing my face. "When we are married, I'll protect you. I promise."

I looked into his eyes and believed him, and for the first time, I didn't correct him.

## 25TH JANUARY

I could already hear the noise of the people gathering without having to open my curtains. I knew it was going to be crazy insane after seeing the lines of people and all the tents yesterday. Not that I was remotely ready for it. How could I be ready? I had a thousand men waiting to make a clay figurine of me and not enough clay to go around. I'd have to look beautiful and charming all day, and all I wanted to do was stay in bed, hiding under my covers. Any second, Dahlia would waltz through the door with yet another dress for me to wear and jabber excitedly about the upcoming event. As if she read my mind, there was a small knock at the door followed by Dahlia calling me lazy and threatening to pour ice water over me to get me out of bed.

"I'm getting up already," I croaked before she had time to carry out her threat.

The dress she'd picked today was a pale powder blue. Not quite dark enough to match my mood, but blue enough to hint at it. I grabbed it from her and pulled it on before she tried wrestling me into the bath.

"This is so exciting," Dahlia enthused.

She clapped her hands together and pushed me into the chair by the window so she could work on my makeup and hair. I reached forward to open the curtains, but she batted them out of my hands.

"Don't spoil the surprise," she admonished. "You'll get to see it all later."

"Great!" I muttered, lacking any enthusiasm. The only good thing, as far as I could see, about the next three days was the fact that I wouldn't have to speak to Caspian. It meant that, at least, I could eat meals in peace without having to worry about his company. He was staying in one of the huge tents that had been arranged for the competitors. I didn't get the feeling that Caspian was one to stay in tents as a rule. Plus, it was freezing cold outside. I allowed myself a little smile at the thought of Caspian freezing his bits off in the tent. I couldn't see him being too happy about molding clay either. He just wasn't the artistic type, and he would hate getting his hands or clothes dirty.

I swallowed back a laugh as Dahlia pulled my hair into a high up ponytail.

Half an hour and one rushed breakfast later, and I was due to go outside.

A trumpet fanfare sounded out as my father took my hand in the entrance hall to the castle.

"Ready?" he asked, squeezing my hand.

I nodded, my stomach in knots. I wasn't ready, but I never would be. This was an echo of what my father thought was to come with my wedding next week. This was practically a trial run for him. He thought he would be escorting me out to adoring crowds then too.

Outside, a long walkway with high fences had been erected out to the pastures where the first leg of the competition would take place. It meant that the crowds hadn't seen us yet, and I could walk in quietness. The calm before the storm.

I gripped my father's hand as we rounded the corner into what I could only describe as a huge stadium. One of the palace staff greeted us and showed us the way to our seats up some stairs at the back. Still, no one had seen us. My father held me back before a pair of curtains in front of us opened.

"You ok?"

I nodded and faced forward. Faced toward my future, whatever that would be.

The trumpet fanfare started again, and my heart provided a handy percussion accompaniment.

The curtains parted, and the roar that happened afterward deafened me with its magnitude. The whole stand shook as thousands of people stood and clapped at our entrance. Two golden thrones had been placed for us high up in the middle of the stand, and a pang of sadness filled me when I realized one was not for my mother, but for me.

I walked silently to the throne and waved, plastering a fake smile to my face as the crowd went wild.

Next to me, sat Remy and beyond him, Hollis. To my left was my father's throne, and next to that, Ash gave me a thumbs up. When the noise finally died down, I sat and gazed around the arena. I'd known it was going to be big, but nothing could have prepared me for just how colossal the place was.

"How many people fit in here?" I whispered to my father as a man rode on horseback to the middle of the arena.

"Twenty thousand members of the public have been let in, but I've been told there are thousands more outside. A thousand men can fit in the center of the arena to fulfill the tasks."

The crowd went silent as a man dressed in a ringmaster's costume on a horse trotted into the arena. He did a lap as an excited buzz filled the stadium. The crowd went wild as he jumped up on the back of the horse, which continued to trot despite the man standing on its back.

"Ladies and Gentlemen," he began as the horse obediently trotted around in a circle so he could address everyone, "Your Majesty, Your Royal Highnesses. Welcome to the show."

Show? This wasn't supposed to be a show. This was supposed to be an important event. Just as I was thinking that this was being lowered to nothing but entertainment, a group of jugglers dressed in Draconis national costume ran out of a tunnel.

"The Draconis National Circus, ladies and gentlemen," the ringmaster said, before trotting back through the tunnel he'd come from.

My stomach fell as the performers gathered into the middle. They didn't walk or run. They back-flipped and cart-wheeled and juggled their way to the center.

All around me, the crowd lapped it up while I sat further into my seat and pretended I was still in bed, and this was some horrific dream. It wasn't that I didn't like performers. I usually loved anything like this, but my plan of getting this madness over and done with was rapidly falling away from me.

The performers gathered into almost a ball before an explosion ripped through the stadium. My heart leapt into my throat, and a good many of the public screamed before a huge dragon made of fire erupted from the performers. It was all part of the show, but it amazed me how real it all looked. To the sound of drums, the fire dragon flew around the stadium, supported by the performers underneath to whoops and hollers coming from the delighted crowd. Even I, who had not wanted any of this sat on the edge of my seat, waiting to see what would happen next. Beside me, Remy stood up in his seat, shouting "dra'a" as the performers passed us.

The percussion increased in pace, building up the tension before the dragon erupted in flames, and the performers collectively danced, pirouetted, and backflipped into a line. They bowed down to my father...or to me. I stood and clapped, feeling that my day might go better than expected.

How bad could it be? It might be quite nice to watch a thousand men trying to recreate my likeness out of clay. The performers left as the ringmaster came back upon his horse.

"And now for the main event. The reason you are all here. The first competition for the Princess Azia's hand in marriage."

I offered up a shy smile as twenty thousand pairs of eyes swiveled my way.

"Please welcome our contestants."

Another cheer went up as the men began to pour out. I sat, literally on the edge of my seat, craning to see the competitors. Most of the men came out, their hands held aloft, fist-bumping the sky, and generally playing it up for the crowd that was loving it.

It took over fifteen minutes to get all of them in the arena. The floor of the arena filled right to the edges leaving very little space for the clay. I watched as the ringmaster trotted back out through the tunnel, and a pair of doors closed behind him. They would open shortly with the huge amounts of clay needed for them to sculpt with. While I waited, I scanned the men again. I found Caspian quickly even though he was wearing the same red outfit as the rest of the men. He'd hate that. There was nothing Caspian liked more than to feel superior with his spiffy way of dressing. Nevertheless, he seemed happy enough as he waved to the crowd along with the others. A few seats in front of me, I saw the back of Charlotte's head as she stood and waved enthusiastically back. I'd not had a chance to speak with her this morning, but I knew she was more excited than I was about this competition.

The tunnel doors opened again, and I sat back into my seat, more excited than I thought I'd ever be. I reflected that making a sculpture of me would be a rather boring event after the earlier performers, and the crowd would be sorely disappointed with the lack of action in the first part of the competition I'd planned. Not that it really mattered. What mattered was whittling these men down to a hundred for the next part of the competition tomorrow.

If sculpting was the way to do it, then so be it.

I was just thinking with dismay that I wasn't going to see Milo's rendition of me now that he'd left when something orange appeared in the corner of my eye.

Somewhere someone screamed, but this was not the scream of excitement. This was fear.

I did a double-take as the screams became louder and not only from the audience. The men nearest the tunnel surged towards us as the orange thing became clear in my eyesight. It was about as far from a lump of clay as anything could get. With bared teeth and sharp claws, the tiger strolled out into the arena.

"What's this?" My father raged, standing up and thumping his fist on the arm of the throne. "I never agreed to this."

I gulped with fear when I realized I had. Inadvertently, but even so, I'd told Jacob to do what he wanted. I'd not expected him to add a tiger to the mix. It wasn't just one tiger. Behind the first walked a second and a third, and behind that, many more.

"The men are unarmed!" I whispered as my father stalked past me in a hurry.

I could only watch on in horror as the men ran screaming away from the giant cats. Fear gripped me to my chair as more of the hungry beasts walked out. I fearfully scanned the men again as the first tiger pounced. A scream of pain followed by the sound of a growling tiger ripping flesh came to my ears. I didn't count, but there must have been more than a hundred tigers brought into the arena. A hundred tigers looking for their next meal. I was going to murder Jacob myself if my father hadn't already done it.

I wanted to close my eyes, but the horror of what was happening before me left me unable to. People all around me were screaming, some were jeering, and some were actively enjoying the spectacle. Right at the front, the line of judges sat still, seemingly impassive to what was happening to the men in front of them. Jacob must have warned them in advance.

My whole body trembled as the tigers attacked. Chaos abounded below me, but some of the men were escaping through the original tunnel. Many more skirted the edge of the arena doing the best they could to get out before the tigers got them. A hundred tigers, a thousand men. They all had a good chance to escape if they were quick enough. Not even the hungriest tiger could eat ten men. Many of the men tried to pull themselves up over the barrier into the crowd. Some succeeded, but many failed simply because they were not tall enough to reach. Caspian was well over six feet four and could grab the edge and haul himself over, but no matter how hard I looked I couldn't see him in the melee. Andrew, Dahlia's son ran for the tunnel and disappeared down it without getting hurt. At least, Dahlia would be happy with that. Not all the men were so lucky. My eyes drifted to one of the tigers near the tunnel entrance. Its prey was in its sight, but the man chose not to run, not to escape the way Andrew had. My breath caught in my throat when I recognized the curls.

"Milo!" I screamed, my voice being lost to the noise of the crowd.

Hundreds of men ran past him down the tunnel, but he held his ground, watching the tiger intently.

My body trembled as I willed him to run as hundreds of others had. He was standing right next to the tunnel. Why didn't he go? Tears ran down my face as I realized he was doing this for me.

"Please run!" I whispered, barely able to get the words out. I wanted Milo to win, but not like this. I never expected him to put his life on the line for me.

As the men thinned out, I was able to see more clearly. The crowd had gotten over their shock, and now they jeered and booed with as much enthusiasm as they had before. Below me, I saw my father gesturing to Jacob to follow him. Jacob's face held a stern expression as he filed past the seated people to my father. I couldn't hear what my father was saying, but it was clear by his expression that Jacob was getting balled out. I took my eyes from them. What did I care what happened to Jacob? With any luck, my father would have his men throw him over the side so he could taste a little of his own medicine.

With every man that ran past Milo into the tunnel, and with every man that clamored over the side, the ratio of men to tigers lowered. Most of the tigers were now busy shredding their catches, chewing down to the flesh and bones of the men who had dared to enter this stupid competition. Nothing was worth losing one's life over and especially not some silly competition to marry a princess. A princess that never wanted to get married in the first place.

"Get out," I shouted, but Milo couldn't hear me. How could he with the screams and shouts of twenty thousand others all shouting at the same time?

I held my breath as the tiger walked closer to him. His eyes fixed on it, but he didn't move.

"Run, you beautiful idiot," I cried, wringing my hands together in terror. Men kept running past him, but the tiger paid them no mind. He was as fixated on Milo as Milo was on him.

"That tiger's a bit close to Milo, don't you think?" Ash said.

I didn't answer. I was afraid that if I opened my mouth, I'd either scream or throw up. My stomach churned as I itched to do something, but what could I do? Not even my father could stop this madness now. As though he'd known I was thinking about him, he passed me and sat down in his throne.

"I didn't know this was going to happen," he said gruffly to me.

"Can't you stop it?" I cried. Jacob was already walking back to his seat.

My father shook his head. I can't. The tigers are trained to leave the arena at the sound of a whistle. That whistle will only be used when there are about a hundred men left standing in the arena. Those hundred will go on to the next part of the competition."

"But you're the king!" I exclaimed. "Make them sound the whistle!"

He shook his head. "I've spoken to Jacob. He kept this from me, but he had good reason. He says that there has been news on the grapevine that the people are ready to revolt. They are upset with the way I've been running the kingdom over the past few weeks. They are upset that my men have been out searching for spindles, they are upset that I built a wall to keep people off the fire mountains but did nothing to keep the dragons from coming down the mountains."

"They are dragons. They can fly. How are you supposed

to keep them from coming down? Anyway, you already knew about this. Jacob is the one who planned the revolt."

" Jacob set up meetings with the ringleaders in the revolt. He promised them this in exchange for keeping their peace. There is nothing more I can do. It's out of my hands. If we do what you wanted to do and have the men answer quiz questions and make statues, we will be overthrown. If that happens, Draconis will be without a royal family to lead it, and we will not have the money needed to keep bringing doctors up here."

"We don't need doctors!" I screamed at him. "She is under a curse. No doctor will be able to save her. Why are you letting Jacob blackmail you? Milo is out there... Your friend Caspian is out there. "

He looked me dead in the eye, sadness clouding his expression. "I know that, but they can keep her alive until we find someone who can break this curse. I can't lose her, Azia."

My heart broke at his words, but he was putting my mother's life up in exchange for everyone's out there, including Milo's and Caspian's.

"You are sacrificing other lives for her. She would never want you to do that."

"We'll never know, will we. Not unless she wakes up." He stood from his throne and walked back down the rows of people. This time when he walked down the stairs, he never came back.

My heart pounded wildly as I turned back to the arena. Milo was gone. I stood up to get a better view as tears poured down my face. I found him. He was still in the arena, but he'd moved. Unfortunately, the tiger had moved too. It stalked around him, moving from side to side, hemming Milo in against the fence separating him from the crowd.

"Jump over the fence," I murmured, but I knew he wouldn't. He kept his back to it as the tiger drew ever closer.

It reared itself, readying to pounce, and still, Milo didn't move. There was only one way for him to go, and that was up the fence behind him, but he didn't make to turn; he just stood there.

Bile rose in my throat as I saw the one person I could ever love inches from death. I cried out again, but my voice was lost in the shrill sounding out of a whistle.

I began to breathe again as the tigers, including the one ready to pounce at Milo, turned and prowled out of the tunnel, leaving those still standing to fight another day.

"Thank you," I mouthed to whatever god was listening. I'd never been religious, but as I was putting all my trust in the fact that Morpheus existed, it stood to reason I could do the same about the other gods too. I'd pray to anyone who would listen to keep Milo safe, and now he was. The first part of the competition was over, and Milo had escaped unscathed.

As I was getting my breath back, the doors to the tunnel opened again, and a number of people with stretchers came out to pick up the injured and the dead.

"I wonder if they are disqualified if they are injured," Ash said.

I turned to him. "For their sake, I really hope they are."

This was only day one. I couldn't keep to the hope that tomorrow would bring a day of figuring out a puzzle. If Jacob had anything to do with it, things were only going to get worse.

As though my mind was being read, the tunnel doors opened again, and the men with stretchers ran from the arena as the contestants who had exited ran back in. I 'd thought that was it, that the madness was over. I couldn't have been more wrong.

I almost fainted when I saw what came out next. Where the tigers had been, now, a hundred lions took their place. They looked no less hungry and mean than the tigers, but now, there were fewer men to each lion. To make matters worse, the doors through which the men had been able to escape earlier had now closed behind them.

The screams and cheers intensified as the world spun around me.

I pulled in a huge breath and steadied myself as dizziness raged within me. If my father wouldn't deal with this, I would.

"Where are you going?" Hollis asked as I edged past him and Remy.

"I'm going to put a stop to this," I replied through gritted teeth.

Running back through the curtain, I took three steps at a time and almost barrelled into Jacob, who stood up when he saw me coming.

"Stop this. Stop it now!" I screamed at him.

"I'm afraid I can't do that, but don't worry. The crowd is loving it. It's the event of the century. People will be talking about this for years."

"I don't give a shit about the crowd," I said, eliciting a gasp from one of the other judges, a young woman in her mid-twenties who probably was the head-teacher Caspian had mentioned.

"What?" I snapped at them. "You are happy to watch innocent men being torn apart, but you get offended when a princess says shit?"

She turned berry red and moved her eyes back to the nightmare in the arena.

"There's no use talking to the judges like that," Jacob grunted. "They aren't to blame. If I remember, this whole debacle was your idea in the first place."

"Not like this, though. I was going to have them make a sculpture, and you know it."

"Now look here," he said, pushing his ugly face into mine.

"No one wants to come out and watch thousands of men make a sculpture of a narcissistic princess. They are here because of this." he swept his hand out behind him. "And if they are here watching this, it means they are not planning to overthrow your father. Now, if you'd prefer, I can call the lions off, but it would mean the people will leave early and get restless. Maybe they'll go home and organize a revolution. All twenty thousand of them."

He grinned at me, knowing he'd backed me into the same corner, he'd backed my father into. But there was one difference between me and my father. I wasn't scared about being overthrown. My only fear was for Milo, who was locked in an arena with lions who wanted nothing more than to feast on his body.

"Do it!" I commanded. "Call them off. I don't care about your threats. Just put an end to this."

The smug grin left his face, but I stood tall, my hands on my hips. I wasn't going to back down.

He stamped his feet on the ground, his fists clenched by his side, but he didn't move. I ripped the whistle from around his neck, breaking the chain holding it and putting it to my lips. Before I'd had the chance to blow, another whistle sounded. Someone else had finished the competition. I turned my head to see why. There were only a hundred men left standing. A hundred men and a hundred well-fed lions. The tunnel gates opened for the last time, and the lions trooped out. I scanned the men, terror filling my very soul that I'd not find Milo, but there he was, mercifully, unscathed. Seconds later, the second wave of people with stretchers came out to mop up the mess left behind. Blood splattered the sand-covered floor, making me feel sick to my stomach. I flung Jacob's necklace back at him and hurled myself over the fence, much to the excitement of the already over-excited crowd.

Milo was much easier to see now that the men had thinned out so much. I raced across the arena to him, not caring who was watching, but before I was halfway across, someone grabbed me. It didn't matter who it was, they were stopping me from getting to Milo, and I needed to speak to him. I needed to tell him that I was wrong. I needed to tell him that I loved him.

The man holding me back turned out to be one of my father's guards. As he was much bigger than me and armed with a sword, I had no choice but to watch as Milo and the others were ushered out of the arena.

"Milo!" I screamed in frustration. I thought he saw me and turned his head to me, but just like that, he was gone. He disappeared into the tunnel with the other ninety-nine men who would have to go through this nightmare again tomorrow. As the last of the men left the arena, I caught sight of the back of Caspian's head. So he'd made it through to the next round too. I knew he would. Still, I felt a moment of unexpended relief that he was alive. Despite everything, I'd actually grown fond of the jerk.

That night, I headed straight for bed. There was no point in going to see my father, nor was there any point going to the castle's admin office. I didn't even want to know what tomorrow would bring, because nothing I could say or do would stop it. Like everything else in my life recently, I was powerless to make any change. In my room, I looked out of the window to the pasture. To the right of the arena was the huge tent where Milo would be spending the night. I wondered what was going through his mind and whether he was as scared as I was at what tomorrow would bring.

## 26TH JANUARY

I was in no mood for company, but I'd not eaten anything since breakfast the previous day, and my stomach was threatening to implode if I didn't eat soon. I walked wearily down to the dining room to find only Charlotte there, eating her breakfast.

"You've just missed everyone," she exclaimed. "Well, your brothers. Your father didn't come for breakfast at all."

"I bet he didn't," I said, pulling a plate toward myself and heaping it with pastries and cold meats.

"I saw that Milo got through," she said. "Caspian, too," she added.

"Yes, but how many didn't get through? How many died just for the chance to marry me? The whole thing is a crock." I slammed the butter onto the bread, spreading it so violently it made a hole in the bread.

"They knew what they were getting into," Charlotte pointed out.

"No, they didn't," I argued, though I don't know why. Charlotte had nothing to do with this. I needed to take my frustration out on someone, and she was the only one there. I pulled the Sentinel towards me and held it up so she could see. A photo of one of the men staring down a tiger filled the front page. "They printed the competition I gave them. These men thought they were going to be making a small statue." I threw the paper back down on the table where it landed on the papers from the other kingdoms. I pulled out the paper below it. The Atlantice Conch. I was on the front cover of that one. Someone had taken a photo of me being held back by the guard when I'd jumped over the fence.

I sighed and threw that one down too. I didn't even want to go through the other kingdoms' papers. The whole thing was embarrassing enough as it was. I didn't need to read about it.

"I don't suppose you know what today's competition is going to be, do you?" I asked. There wasn't a chance that my fantastic puzzle was going to be used.

"I don't know," Charlotte said, shrugging her shoulders. "I only hope it's not as brutal as yesterday. I almost had a heart attack when one of the lions ran over to Caspian. He would have gotten him too if he'd not performed a spell."

I raised my eyebrows as Charlotte brought her hand up to her mouth.

"I wasn't supposed to say that. Please don't be mad."

So Caspian was using magic. It figured. I'd put a blanket ban on all magic, but since when did Caspian listen to a word I said and followed my rules? Precisely never, that's when, and I guessed I couldn't hope for him to start now.

"Don't worry about it," I reassured her. "I don't even care anymore. I just want Milo to come out of this alive, I don't care who wins now, not even if it's Caspian. I should have married him right at the start and avoided all this."

Charlotte nodded, but I could see in her eyes that she didn't agree with me. Of course, she didn't. She wanted to marry Caspian herself. I sighed and bit into my soggy bread.

After breakfast, I waited for my father to walk me outside to the arena, but he was nowhere to be seen.

"Dahlia, do you know where my father is?" I asked impatiently.

"Actually, I do. He's asked me to walk out with you. He says he's not feeling well and not up to watching more of what happened yesterday. Not that I can blame the man. It made me sick to my stomach too."

My heart leapt into my throat. "He's not well?"

Dahlia took my hand as the doors to the castle opened. "I think he doesn't want to watch his subjects being killed. I know his situation. He's letting the competition continue because he doesn't want the kingdom to go to wrack and ruin. The competitors are collateral damage in this whole thing."

She tsked and shook her head.

"I forgot to ask you yesterday. How is Andrew?" Andrew was Dahlia's son and the light of her life.

"He's fine. Nearly wet himself yesterday when the tigers came out, though. The kid couldn't get away fast enough. I told him not to enter, but would he listen to me? Oh, no. At least, he's out of harm's way from whatever monstrosity Jacob's planned for today's entertainment. He's at home licking his wounded pride and probably eating all my homemade pies. Come on. we can't put this off any longer."

The pair of us walked out to another trumpet fanfare. As long as I lived, I'd associate the sound of trumpets with the stench of death, and I had a feeling that today was only going to cement that connection.

We walked down the same covered pathway we had done before, ending at the same staircase. I knew where to go without help, but I couldn't let Dahlia's hand go. She was my emotional crutch, and without Milo by my side, she was all I had. After climbing the stairs, I stood behind the curtains waiting for them to open. As they had yesterday, they opened, but to my surprise, the other half of the stadium was no longer there. I'd not checked out of my window this morning and so I'd not seen the massive amount of work that must have happened throughout the night. Dahlia practically dragged me to my throne as the fanfare started again. The view of the Fire Mountains took my breath away, even through the soft snowflakes that had begun to fall. Looking left and right, I could see that the stadium had been extended outwards and was now a half-oval shape open at one side. My stomach turned as I wondered what exactly this meant. What could they possibly need more space for? They'd managed to fit a thousand or so men in the arena yesterday, along with numerous lions and tigers. Today, there were only a hundred men to fit in. There was no way they were going to spend the day doing a puzzle, no matter how tricky.

"Good morning, Your Highnesses, Ladies and Gentlemen," began the ringmaster, sending the audience into silence. Beside me, Remy and Hollis looked on intently, while at the other side of my father's empty throne sat Ash. Right behind me with her hand on my shoulder, sat Dahlia. The ringmaster was back on his horse, but now, he carried an umbrella to protect him from the snow. He trotted up and down, repeating his greeting for the benefit of the people furthest away.

My nerves tightened as he came back to us. Behind him, the men left were brought out, lining up. Picking Milo out was much easier today. He was about a third of the way along the line, and when the Ringmaster introduced the men, he bowed along with everyone else. It broke my heart that he didn't look my way once. Caspian, I noticed stood right in the middle, and unlike Milo, who looked anywhere but me, had his eyes trained on mine. He gave me a wave when he saw I was looking. The rest of thc men had a variety of expressions ranging from out-and-out fear to excitement of the unknown. I wondered if they'd feel so excited once this part of the competition started because I doubted all these men would return home to their families after this day was done. The organizers had done a good job of covering up the blood spilled yesterday, but it was still visible in the darker shades of sand that covered the arena floor. I only wished it would snow harder so it would cover the dark patches completely. Every one of the men carried a sword.

The ringmaster waited for the noise from the crowd to die down before speaking again.

"Today, these fine men while be whittled down from a hundred to ten. Only ten men will be able to go through to the final round to compete for the princess's hand in marriage. The rest will go home tonight with the knowledge that they had done their best but ultimately were not good enough."

Would they, though? I wondered. Would they go home tonight, or would they end their day, lifeless in a wooden box?

A woman in a beautiful dress walked out into the open arena. She carried something in her hands that she passed to the ringmaster. It looked suspiciously like...

"This," the ringmaster said, holding the object aloft, "is a wooden egg. Ten of them have been hidden up the Fire Mountains behind me. Each has a number etched into it. The number corresponds to the order in the man finding the egg will complete tomorrow's task. In one minute exactly, I will blow a whistle, and the men will race to find these eggs and bring them back. Remember, there are only ten. They have been hidden amongst the real dragon eggs up there. Are you ready?"

Fear filled me as the hundred men readied themselves for the race. Sending a hundred men up the mountain would spoil everything I'd worked toward. The peace between the dragons and the humans was tenuous at best. This would destroy everything.

"No!" I screamed as he blew the whistle, drowning out my voice.

The men dashed to the base of the mountain at roughly the same speed I ran downstairs to confront Jacob. Two burly guards stood at each side of the judges' table, anticipating my reaction. They both stood to attention as I approached.

"What are you playing at?" I screamed at Jacob. "You can't have a hundred men going up the mountain. They'll upset the dragons."

This was his revenge for the other day when he'd not been able to kill any of the dragons, He'd done this on purpose as an excuse. Dragonfire, I hated that man.

Jacob checked that his guards were nearby before he spoke. "So? It wouldn't be much of a competition if we buried the eggs in the snow, would it? Besides, who cares if a few dragons get killed along the way?"

All around us, the audience had stopped watching the men, and now, all eyes were on me to see what my reaction would be. I'd caused enough of a stir yesterday by jumping over the fence separating the audience from the arena floor. No doubt, everyone was wondering if I'd do the same thing again today. Thoughts of Milo getting fried and my friends Nyre, Vasuki, and Emba being hurt, spurred me into action. I turned on my heel and ran for the exit to the arena. I didn't get very far before Jacob's guards grabbed hold of me, pulling me back to Jacob.

"Princess, princess, princess," he said smugly, rubbing his hands together. "You caused a scene yesterday. I don't think your father would be happy if you did the same again today, would he?"

I gritted my teeth. "You don't care what my father wants. He wouldn't want this." I held my hand out to the base of the mountains where the competitors were running.

He gave me a smug smile. "I don't like holding you against your will so publicly, but if I tell everyone you are planning on going up the mountain, they will understand why I had to stop you. No one wants the kingdom's favorite princess to get hurt, especially so close to her wedding day."

"I'm not going up the mountain, you imbecile. I'm going to speak to my father."

I hoped he'd believe my lie. My father was no use in this, and Jacob knew it.

"Fine," he said, nodding at the guards who let me go. "Good luck. You might want to be back before nightfall. The action will start at twilight when the men get back."

Behind him, the men had already reached the wall my father had erected. Ladders stood against it at ten feet intervals. There were only twenty or so of them, so some of the men had to wait their turn, but it took less than two minutes for every man to jump over to the other side.

Leaving Jacob and the arena behind, I raced back to the castle. It was completely deserted, thanks to the event out front. Most of the staff had been given leave to go watch the competition, which meant it was extremely easy to slip through unnoticed and out through the back garden gate to the woods. Once I was through, I used my magic to call for Nyre. I was far enough away from the stadium that she could come down the mountain and not be seen. She was small enough to pass for a large bird of prey from a distance, even if she was seen. I only hoped she'd be able to get away from the other dragons. I'd left Vasuki on good terms, but she had been hurt, and he was her father. I knew how protective my own father could be.

I didn't need to worry because she soon appeared, a little purple dot flying through the snow.

"Nyre!" I cried out when she landed on the ground beside me. "Are you ok? I'm so sorry about what Jacob did to you."

She nodded and held out her wing. There was a nip out of the very edge of it. I brought her into a quick hug. She pulled back and positioned herself as though she was about to shift.

"No," I shouted. "Stop. I need you to take me up the mountain...now!"

She must have heard the urgency in my voice because she jumped quickly onto my shoulder and pulled me into the air. My breath was lost to the bitterly cold air, and goosebumps appeared on my arms as we flew upwards.

In the distance, the crowd in the stadium cheered the men along. The sound was soon drowned out to the silence of the snowfall. We flew through the clouds to the peaks, and Nyre dropped me in the same nest I'd first come to. Only then, did she change.

"What's up?"

"We're in trouble." I wheezed as a blast of cold air hit the back of my throat. I wrapped my arms around myself to keep warm. The dress I'd put on this morning was not nearly warm enough for standing on the top of a mountain in the middle of winter. "The competition...The castle admin staff...Jacob has had fake eggs planted up here. There are a hundred men on their way up here now to take them back."

Nyre's eyes widened. "They can't. Our eggs are up here. How did they even get them into our nests in the first place?"

"I don't know. They did it last night under the cover of darkness. I need to see your father. He needs to be made aware."

Nyre shook her head violently. "No. He'll freak out. He's been patient, but he won't like this. You promised him that no one would come up the mountain. You've promised him a few times, Azia."

"I know I did," I said, feeling sick to my stomach. "I didn't ask them to come up. I tried to stop it, but I can't. They are already on their way. Can't we just fly around the nests and collect the real dragon eggs and take them down to your village? Even if it's just for a few hours."

I already knew her answer. I'd asked Vasuki the same thing, but I was clutching at straws.

She folded her arms and glared at me. I could understand her anger at me. I deserved it. ever since I'd first journeyed up the Fire Mountain, there'd been nothing but trouble.

"No. The eggs have to be up here. They are too fragile to move, and I can't risk it. Besides, the mothers of each egg will be roosting on them, keeping them warm. Do you want to explain to them that we need to endanger their children's lives for some stupid human competition?"

She stamped her foot in the snow. At any other time, the gesture would look adorable on her, but now, it broke my heart and sent me into a panic.

"I'm sorry."

"Look. No point saying sorry," she huffed. "We need to fix this, and we need to do it quickly before my father finds out."

I thought for a moment.

"We need to figure out how castle staff got the eggs up here. If you say that the mothers are protecting the nests, how, in all the kingdoms, would they have been able to get the fake eggs in there? Are there many other empty nests like this one?"

Nyre shook her head impatiently. "No. This is the only one. The rest are occupied. I guess they might have got the fake eggs in while the mothers were feeding?"

I took a deep breath and considered my options. I didn't really have any. Either we tell Vasuki and start a war or get those eggs before the hundred men climbed to the top of the mountain. Neither option sounded promising, especially seeing as I was already freezing cold from the weather.

"Ok," I said, coming up with a plan. "We have time on our side. It's a five-hour climb to the mountain tops. These men will probably be faster than me, so we can lower it to four. The weather might slow them down, but I don't want to factor that in and be wrong. Let's aim to get those wooden eggs in the next four hours. We'll get each one while the mother is feeding. You can fly me down, and we can throw each one at the men, so hopefully, they'll see that they don't have to go up the mountain any further."

Nyre glared at me as though I was insane, and I probably was.

"You want to steal eggs from the dragon mother's nests? Do you know how insane that sounds? You might think Darius is an angry fellow, but let me tell you, he's nothing to a mother dragon. They are fierce!"

I nodded. "I'm aware of the insanity of the situation, but to sit back and watch everyone getting hurt would be much worse. I'm doing this, Nyre, with or without your help. I'd prefer with..."

I could have compelled her to do it, but I needed her to make the decision on her own.

I waited for her to decide. Finally, she wavered. "Okay, but we can't touch any of the real eggs. They might be dragons, but they are babies, and they are precious."

"Agreed, "I said, throwing her a smile. I'd never taken her to be the motherly type, and here she was, clucking over some eggs.

When I'd come up with the plan, I'd thought we'd easily be able to fly from nest to nest, grabbing each wooden egg and hurling it down the mountain. What I hadn't counted on was the fact that none of these dragon mamas were hungry.

They paid us no mind as we flew over their heads. I was no threat to them, and neither was Nyre, or so they all thought. And yet, none of them moved.

"Can't we just ask them to move for some other reason?" I shouted up to Nyre when we were out of earshot of the dragons. Nyre couldn't speak to me in her dragon form, but she didn't need words to convey the message. She shook her head and glared at me again. So we waited....and waited...and waited. If I used my magic to force them to move, they would fly straight down to the village and tell Vasuki the second the spell broke. Just as I had let Nyre do things her own way, so I had to wait for the mama dragons.

"Why aren't they moving?" I whined a few hours later. I could no longer feel my toes; I was that cold, and flying around in the talons of a dragon was not making the situation any better. I'd just about given up on the whole thing when the first dragon took off into the air. She soared away majestically, her lemon yellow wings out fully as she skimmed the mountain tops, thankfully, in the opposite direction to the men coming up the mountain on the other side. This had been something else I'd thought about in the hours I'd been pointlessly flying around. What if one of the dragon mamas decided to go and find food at this side of the mountain? I didn't know what they ate, but judging by the bones left in the nests I'd seen, I was guessing they survived on a diet of mountain goat and the odd cow. Now while they'd have to fly further afield for a cow, there were plenty of mountain goats on the side of the mountain facing the castle. I tried putting the thought from my mind as Nyre swooped me lower towards the empty nest.

Finding the wooden egg was easy. Despite it being practically the same size as the other eggs, it was smooth in texture and not mottled like the others. Also, it was made out of wood and had the number seven engraved on it. As Nyre dangled me above it, I pulled it out slowly, careful not to disrupt any of the other eggs. It came out nicely, and Nyre was able to fly me down the mountain. The clouds were low in the sky, so the arena below us was hidden. I couldn't help but think that it must be very boring to watch from the ground when all anyone would be able to see was clouds. Not that Jacob cared. He spoke of spectacle and excitement, but he just wanted the dragons dead so he didn't have to send his men out to build any more wall, that and the fact that without the dragons around, he'd be able to come up later and steal the real dragon eggs without a fight.

It was both good and bad. The men were still below the cloud line, which meant that none of them could see what I was up to. This was good because they wouldn't head back down the mountain and tell Jacob, just for him to send more men up to fight. It was also bad because I couldn't see them and if I couldn't see them, it meant Nyre couldn't see them either. If we waited for the men to climb above the cloud, we'd run out of time. As it was, the hours of time I thought we had to collect the eggs were quickly decreasing, thanks to the mother dragons.

Nyre dipped into the clouds. Instantly, the coldness I felt worsened as dampness was added to the mix.

As she flew, I scanned the ground for any of the men. Finally, we saw one. I didn't recognize him, but he looked extremely fit. I whistled loudly, and as he looked up, I threw the egg at him. He caught it and gazed down at it as though he couldn't believe his luck. When he thought enough to look to see where it had come from, Nyre and I were already up through the clouds.

Over the course of two hours, we managed to collect seven more of the wooden eggs easily. Much more easily than I had first thought. Each time we grabbed one, it was thrown to one lucky man who could then turn around and march home. With each egg we threw, the men climbed higher and higher up the mountain, and with it, the fear that we might not make it. My plan was to tell all the men that there were no eggs left once they broke through, but as I threw the eighth egg, it was beginning to look like it wasn't true. The last two mothers were still sitting comfortably upon their nests and not looking like they planned to move any time soon. All I could do was watch impatiently, waiting for the first man to break through the clouds and get to him before the other dragons saw him. My nerves were frayed by the time the ninth dragon finally left her roost to feed. Nyre sprinted to the nest, but I could see we'd left it too late. The men were already appearing through the cloud just fifty meters or so below us.

I hurled the ninth egg down to them, hoping one would catch it, but once they saw what it was, they made a dash for it. I counted fifteen of them brawling for the egg on a precarious ledge.

"Do something!" I screamed to Nyre, but what could she do? She was tiny and had been working enough to haul me about all morning. If she flew down to them, the surprise would surely topple them from the edge.

And then, that wasn't my problem anymore.

As I'd been watching on with horror at the men fighting over the egg, I'd taken my eyes from the tenth dragon. She was way off in the distance, and so I'd paid her no mind, but it was hard to ignore the sharp blast of fire erupting from her mouth.

Nyre swerved around towards her before I had the chance to ask her. When she flew, it was almost like we were one. She understood where I wanted to go instinctively, and I knew where she was going. It might have been something to do with the dragon magic I held. Not that it was going to be much help now. I could summon the dragons. If I summoned the mother dragon to me, she would be compelled to come. It would save the lives of the men I could see climbing up the mountain below her, but it wouldn't save anything else. She would report me to Vasuki, and I'd have all the dragons out on the mountain.

"Stop!" I demanded of the men below her. The ones that were still alive. The charred remains of two of the men smoked on the mountain, and the smell of burned flesh filled the air. My stomach churned as I tried to keep my composure.

Nyre dropped me to the ground roughly halfway between the dragon and the charred bodies. with my fingers crossed that the dragon wouldn't flame me, I addressed the men. I shouted loud enough so the men fighting over the ninth egg could hear too.

"There is only one egg left. I've been throwing them to the men who beat you up here. This dragon behind me holds the last one, but if any of you step closer, I will ask her to flame you all alive."

Behind me, I could hear the beat of Nyre's wings as she hovered between me and the mama dragon.

"Go back down the mountain. I will not have you harm this dragon or any other. This is a mother protecting her young. As the Princess of Draconis, I command it."

I stood tall, as the men wavered. Some turned to leave, but almost as soon as I thought I'd diffused the situation, some of the men charged me. All hell broke loose as the men that had joined a competition to marry me were now scrambling towards me with their swords out. I was above them. If I had my sword and it was one on one, I could have beaten them easily. As it was, I had no sword, was wearing a dress, and couldn't feel my own fingers. More than ten chased toward me. As the first one reached me, I kicked out, sending him reeling down the mountain. The scream he emitted as he fell through the clouds would haunt me, but I had no time to worry. Another one was rapidly approaching. I fumbled backward, climbing up the mountain to get away from him. But I was heading toward a much more deadly foe. The mother dragon had been watching with interest, but as I turned to her, I could see the nervousness in her eyes. She wasn't scared to kill. She was a dragon . It was in her nature. She was scared to kill me. The Queen of Dragons. I was the one getting between her and the men she thought wanted to steal her babies.

I had no choice. The men had made their decision and would have to suffer the consequences. I couldn't save them now.

"Go!" I pleaded with them one last time as I stepped aside to let the dragon breath flames down the mountain.

And then something happened that had me rooted to the spot. Milo appeared below them . If I moved now, Milo would be killed alongside these strangers. Milo, who was only in this competition for me despite the fact he thought I was dating Caspian.

My heart lurched as I watched him climb around the other men, but it was too late. He wouldn't be able to save any of us.

A flash of purple caught my eye as Nyre flew down the mountain and plucked him up in her talons. She dropped him beside me as the first man caught hold of my ankle.

"Don't you dare touch her," he screamed, bringing his foot down hard on the man's hand. The man screamed and let go, dropping his sword before falling ten feet or so below us. Milo drew his sword and faced the men.

"If one of you lays a finger on her or even thinks about harming this dragon or her eggs, I'll kill you all. With my bare hands if I have to."

But he didn't have to. He had his sword, and he was above

them. He had every advantage. I watched on as he fought them one by one. A couple were picked off by Nyre, who dodged their swords and flung them down the mountain. Behind me, the dragon mother bellowed. I turned to see one of the men climbing into her nest. The fear in the eyes of the dragon was obvious. She wanted to kill this man, but indecision had her rooted to the spot.

"Kill him!" I shouted out. She didn't have to breathe fire. She could chew his head off or swipe him with her talons. But I could see that what was stopping her was her eggs. She didn't want to move for fear of trampling them. As I watched, another man pulled himself up into her nest, spurred on by the bravery of the first and the fact that the dragon was stock still, paralyzed with fear.

If she couldn't do anything, I could. I picked up the sword dropped by the man earlier and sprinted upwards while Nyre and Milo fought the men below.

They were coming thick and fast now, more of them emerging from the cloud, eager to fight it out over the remaining wooden egg.

"I'm here to help you," I said to the terrified dragon. She nodded with tears in her eyes. If only people understood that dragons were not the terrifying creatures they were made out to be as long as they were not provoked.

I patted her snout then turned towards the men. They'd both seen the wooden egg and were approaching it quickly. I ran towards them, my sword out ahead of me. I'd trained my whole life for this moment. The first went down quickly. He'd not expected the princess to fight him and so had not defended when 'd stabbed him right in his heart. He died with an expression of shock on his face. The second had a couple more seconds to ready himself, and so I had to be better. I had to be better than him because this was a fight to the death, and we both knew it. He didn't care that I was the princess, nor the prize in this stupid competition anymore. His focus was on winning, and that was all that mattered. I fought bravely, but he was good. I struggled to attack and could only defend. It wasn't helping that I couldn't feel my hands, and the cold weather combined with the ridiculous dress slowed me down. I moved backward with each thrust of his sword. He hesitated for a second, and I managed to get a swipe in, but he was quick to regain his momentum and attacked again. My back struck the edge of the nest. This was it. I kill him, or he would kill me. I defended each of his attacks, but with my hands being numb, I couldn't move as quickly as I would like. He reached back and swiped my sword right out of my hand, leaving me weaponless and hopeless.

I pressed my back into the edge of the nest and waited for death to come. This was it. I closed my eyes and waited, but then the sound of crunching bones had me opening them. I heaved as I saw the sight before me. A pair of bloody legs stood in front of me, the torso and head ripped from them. The legs fell over as I caught sight of the dragon having a fine feast of warrior torso for dinner. I heaved then threw up over the side.

Behind me, something grabbed me and hoisted me into the air. At first, I thought it was the dragon, but then I realized it was only Nyre. She plucked me from the nest and began the flight back to the castle. As we descended the mountain, I got a peek at the other dragons approaching the nest of the tenth dragon from the other side of the mountain. Hundreds of them. I recognized Vasuki at the front.

"Stop!" I murmured, but it was too late. She usually obeyed my wishes, but I was too tired and cold to shout louder. She was ignoring me anyway. My dragon magic was at an all-time low, and I had nothing left in me to give. She didn't drop me at the back of the woods, but in the castle garden, before flying off again.

"Stop!" I shouted again. "Milo is up there. The dragon mama!" She ignored me and disappeared into the clouds as the world began to spin. I fell to the ground only vaguely aware that some of the castle staff had run out to me.

I awoke hours later in my own bed. "As soon as my eyes fluttered open, Dahlia shouted to someone to bring me soup. One of the castle staff must have run to pass on the message because she closed the door and ran over to my bed."

"I've been so worried. You silly girl. What did you think you were doing?"

"Milo?" I croaked.

Just then there was a knock at the door. As Dahlia was busy fending off whoever was at my door, I used the opportunity to jump out of bed and check the scene from my bedroom window. From this distance, I couldn't see much, but the low level of light told me I'd been out for hours. Torches lit the arena in the dim twilight. Without looking back, I opened the window and standing on the ledge, compelled Nyre to come and get me. Behind me, I heard a commotion and the clattering of a bowl on the stone floor. A quick look back told me Dahlia had seen what I was up to. The clattering was my soup. She dashed toward me, followed quickly by a kitchen servant and Jack. As though everything was happening in slow motion, I leapt outward as Dahlia reached the window. Her fingers brushed my ankle, but it was too late. I was already falling toward the cobbles in the courtyard below.

Dahlia's scream filled the night. Inches above the courtyard, Nyre swooped in as I'd known she would and pulled me into the air.

I'd known she would catch me in time. We were so in tune with each other that leaping from my bedroom window was not the feat of insanity it must have appeared to be to anyone watching.

I'd expected Nyre. What I hadn't expected was a fleet of dragons following in her wake. We flew through the air, Nyre and I in the lead with a V-shape of dragons behind us. So much for Vasuki not finding out.

Nyre swooped into the arena.

The men that had already managed to get back scattered as we came to land amid a wave of screams and commotion.

As we landed, only three men ran in our direction. My father, Jacob, and Milo.

Milo ran straight for me, sweeping me off my feet and spinning me around much to the delight of the crowd.

As tears dripped down my face, Milo kissed me. The audience loved it, judging by the oohs and aahs that now took over from the screams of before. My whole world came to a standstill as a wave of happiness overcame me. Someone in the crowd began to clap, quickly followed by others until, like a peal of thunder, the sound engulfed us, surrounded us until, like the beating of my heart, that's all there was. Just Milo and I and the thunderous applause of twenty thousand people, telling me that I'd been right all along. I wanted Milo.

As he pulled away, the grin on his face made me laugh, and my tears turned to tears of happiness.

"Kill them!" Jacob screamed to his men, taking me out of my moment of euphoria. He raised his sword, aiming at the long row of dragons that lined the edge of the arena floor.

"No man and no dragon will die here tonight." My father said, stepping in front of him.

My father looked up and addressed the crowd. Now that they had seen my father, the crowd became silent, eager to see what would happen next.

I held my breath as Vasuki walked forward. As he walked, he shifted into his half-human form. The audience gave a collective gasp when they saw him change. He walked to my father and held out his hand. This time my father shook it.

"This is my friend, Vasuki," My father shouted out to the people. "He and his kind are welcome in Draconis, the kingdom named after them. There will be no more killing. From this moment on, The Fire Mountains are prohibited to all humans by decree of the king. Anyone caught up there without permission from Vasuki or anyone caught with a dragon egg will be punished to the highest degree of the law."

"You can't do that!" Jacob yelled, holding his sword up to Vasuki. "As the king, you can put forward a law, but it has to go through Urbis to get it passed. It could take months. Until then, I am legally allowed to do what I want regarding the dragons."

"That's true," my father answered, pulling his sword, "but you'll have to come through me."

He swiped at Jacob's sword, knocking it away from Vasuki. The crowd went wild, never having seen their king fight before. I held my breath as Jacob lunged at my father. Neither man was wearing armor, and one thrust to the abdomen would kill either one of them. Milo gripped my hand tightly to stop me from running between the fighting men. I guess he knew me too well because, despite the fact I had no sword and was wearing only my nightgown, that's exactly what I wanted to do.

My father was more skilled than I had anticipated. He blocked Jacob's thrusts, parrying and thrusting with his own sword. I could only watch on with bated breath as they danced around each other, fighting in a whirl of speed and flair.

The noise of the crowd increased, and over the deafening roar, I could just make out Remy's voice shouting, Dad!

My father seemed the stronger of the two, but he mistimed his step and fell, allowing Jacob to hold his sword to my father's neck. Milo's grip on my hand loosened as the crowd booed Jacob. I ran toward them, unsure of what to do. Jacob's face was contorted with rage, and he knew as well as I did that he would have to kill my father or lose face. A lifetime in prison awaited him if he carried out the murder of the king, but he was too far gone to stop now. He pulled his sword back, ready to strike, and at that moment, he flew into the air, carried by a dragon with yellow scales. Kuda flew up through the clouds as a cheer erupted through the crowd. I held out my hand and pulled my father up into a standing position.

"The men have been picked," my father addressed the audience. "I think today has been eventful enough. We will see you all back here tomorrow for the final round. Goodnight."

He waved with one hand , taking my hand in his other one. Milo raced over and took my free hand. What did any of us care anymore who knew that I loved Milo? I didn't care. We had only one night left to be together, and I was going to make the most of it.

# 27TH JANUARY

Milo's soft breathing beside me told me that yesterday hadn't just been a wonderful dream. No one had stopped us when we'd walked hand in hand to my room, and though the guard outside had tried, my father had told him to leave us alone.

A small knock on the door had Milo stir, but he didn't awaken. I had a curse on my lips for Dahlia for waking us up. She knew Milo was here. She must have. But when I opened the door, it was only Jack with the morning's breakfast on a tray.

"Dahlia asked me to give these to you," he said gruffly. "She said you might not want to come down for breakfast, so she had it brought up."

He eyed me suspiciously as he handed the tray over. On it were two plates of cold meats and cheese, along with two croissants and a pot of jam. Two cups of coffee and the morning papers took up the rest of the tray. He tried looking over my shoulder to see who was with me, but I managed to close the door before he saw his precious work-mate in my bed. It would blow the poor man's mind, although if he'd had bothered to check the papers on the tray he'd have seen the pair of us kissing on the very front page. I stifled a grin as I thanked him and took the tray, closing the door firmly behind him.

I looked at the front covers of the Draconian Sentinel on the top as I placed the tray on my side of the bed. It was the second time in a week that they'd posted a photo of me kissing someone. I was becoming quite the scandal! Putting the Sentinel to one side, I checked out the covers of the other kingdoms' newspapers. Most had the same or a similar photo with the story of my competition. I was becoming famous in all the other kingdoms. The only cover not to feature me was the Atlantice Conch. It had a story about how things were beginning to change, about a shift in the energy in the water. It felt horribly familiar. I threw the papers down, not really caring. I had better things to think about.

Milo opened his eyes as I slid back into the warm bed beside him. Thankfully, I'd rested the tray beside me because he brought me toward him, catching me in a kiss. My heart beat in triple time as his lips lingered upon mine, and my body danced a whirl as he pulled me closer, our bodies touching.

Last night had been about new beginnings, new feelings, and new experiences. Experiences I desperately needed to feel again, feel for the last time with Milo, because in a few short hours, the last day of the competition would begin.

"I wish this could last forever," Milo said, threading his fingers through mine.

His words were bittersweet. It couldn't last forever. At worst, we had hours; at best, we might be able to sneak time before the wedding. We'd wasted so much time, and now my wedding was almost upon us. A wedding which Milo would definitely not be a part of. He was out of the competition. He'd not managed to bring back an egg. At least, Caspian hadn't managed it either, I'd not even seen him up on the mountain. Not that I cared anymore. I was going to have to marry someone and that someone wasn't Milo. It would be a stranger. Someone I didn't know and had likely only met briefly. It didn't bear thinking about.

"Don't think about it," Milo said as though he could read my mind. "We have some time together. I promise that I won't leave your side for any of it, and when the day comes for you to get married, I'll step back and let you get on with your life."

"What do you mean?"

"I'm going to The Forge and live with my mom."

Tears streamed down my face as I took in his words. I knew it had to happen even before he said it, but hearing it out loud made it all the more real. He was right to go. I wouldn't have been able to bear him being so close to me in the castle while I pretended to be happily married to someone else. It would be impossible for him too. Milo kissed away every tear, and as the tray fell to the floor with a crash, sending cold coffee all over the floor, he pulled me back to him.

The urgency in his touch was apparent. Where last night, he'd traced my skin, giving me goosebumps as we'd taken our sweet time getting to know each other's touch, now with the promise of the competition starting soon, time was a luxury we didn't have. Despite my hope that we might be able to snatch a few secret hours before the wedding next week, it was unlikely. I would need to concentrate on my new fiancée. I blocked it all out as Milo crushed his lips to mine, obliterating every thought. I pressed my body to his and surrendered myself to beautiful oblivion.

~

Light poured into the room filtering through the gauzy curtains, signaling the end of our time together. I kissed Milo softly on the forehead, tasting the salty taste of sweat from our exertions.

"I have to get up," I sighed, glancing at the brightening sky, just peeking through my curtains. "I have to go to the competition. " I'd put it off as long as I could, but the sound of the general hustle and bustle of the castle had been going on for a while, and I knew it wouldn't be long before Dahlia came to fetch me.

Milo didn't stop me climbing out of bed, though the pain in his eyes almost broke my heart. Today was the day I would finally meet my husband to be. I tried not to think about it as I pulled on a dress from my wardrobe. I didn't have Dahlia to help me today, so I picked a dress I thought she might choose and pulled my hair into a high ponytail. The dress I was willing to do, but I wasn't going to spend hours on hair and makeup. My husband to be would just have to take me as I was. He had the advantage of knowing who I was to begin with. I didn't even know that about him.

As I stepped to my door, Milo took hold of my hand.

"You can't come out into public with me," I reminded him. The whole kingdom would see us on the cover of the newspaper this morning, but I couldn't be seen with him again. It wouldn't be fair to the competition winner

"I know," he replied softly, "but I'll be with you every step of the way until then."

I gave him a sad smile as I squeezed his hand. Our time together had been so brief, and it had almost run out. So many regrets ran through my mind as I opened the bedroom door, but sleeping with Milo wasn't one of them. I only wished I'd done it earlier... wished I'd spent more time with him. Jack's face was a picture when he saw who was with me. I gave him a smile and was just about to say something when there was a tap on my window. I turned to see Nyre flapping her wings outside. Running to her, I opened the window. With a wink, she dropped something heavy at my feet before once again taking to the sky. I looked down to find a wooden egg. The same wooden egg I'd protected against the two men in the nest the day before.

"Of course! There was an egg left." I whispered as I picked it up and showed Milo.

"You're still in!" I squealed, jumping up and down.

Milo caught my excitement. "I'll win this thing, Azia. I'll win it for us." He brought his lips to mine, and for the first time since this infernal competition started, I thought I might actually begin to enjoy it.

"You'd better hurry up, lad," Jack said. "They competitors have already been called out."

Milo gave me a grin and took off down the corridor, the egg in his hands.

I found my father in the entrance hall waiting for me to go out with him.

"I'm so proud of you, Azia," he said, taking my hand. "Whatever happens today, I want you to know that."

My heart swelled as I stepped outside. It was too late for my father to call this thing off now, but I knew in my gut that Milo would win. He was an amazing swordsman and the only member of my father's guard to have entered. He was taught by the best, and he'd practiced endlessly with me. Now that Caspian was out of the competition, I had every faith that Milo had it in the bag.

Happiness flowed through me as my father and I ascended the stairs. When the curtain was pulled back, we both headed to our thrones. My brothers were there exactly as they had been for the past two days, with Remy next to me and Ash next to my father. Hollis sat next to Remy, and beyond him, Dahlia sat, giving me a mischievous wink as I passed.

The crowd roared as the ten winners from yesterday were brought onto the field.

Milo came on first, waving at the crowd as though he didn't have a care in the world. In his hand, he carried the egg that Nyre had brought to us, not ten minutes before. A roar filled the arena as he held the wooden egg into the air. He'd gone from a nobody to the kingdom's favorite. The crowd wanted him to win as much as I did. Another nine men trooped out and took their place beside him. Not one of them got the same reaction from the crowd as Milo had. Each of them carried an egg. I scrutinized them one by one as they stood in line. Never had I seen a meaner bunch of men, each burlier than the last. It was only when I came to the last man in line that I let out a gasp of surprise.

"What's Caspian doing here?" I whispered to my father. I was sure he'd not gotten an egg the day before.

"He fought one of the men coming down the mountain with an egg," my father explained as the men took a bow.

Now that Caspian was back in the game, my excitement faded. He was a great swordsman. I'd never once beaten him. I consoled myself with the fact it wasn't me having to fight him. It was Milo, and Milo had beaten him that one time.

The ringmaster lined them up in the order of the numbers on the eggs.

"Today, a new prince will be picked. A man fit to marry the Princess Azia. These ten men have bravely fought tigers and lions and dragons for her hand in marriage. Today, they will only have to fight each other. Each man will be paired up with another. When we have a victor in each pair, the winner will move on to the next round, with the winner being the only man left standing. There are only two ways to win. If your partner dies or if your partner holds his hand up in submission, thus taking himself out of the competition. We will keep going until there is only one man left. Now that you've seen the men, we will have an intermission while they put on their armor. We don't want to make it too easy. While you wait, please welcome the Draconis Opera."

The men walked off as some singers came into the arena. The opera was amazing, but my mind was on other things. Namely Milo and Caspian. I didn't care about the others. I didn't think they would win, but in an ironic twist of fate, it had come down to the two men it had started with. Like it or not, this time next week, I was going to be married to one of them. I just didn't know which one.

Two men came onto the arena floor as the main singer finished her aria. They were covered head to toe in armor, so it was difficult to see who they were. The ringmaster stood them five feet apart and instructed them to draw their swords. My heart was in my mouth as he blew his whistle, and the men began to fight. I knew both Milo's and Caspian's style, which meant I thought that neither of these men was either of them. I wasn't a hundred percent confident, though, and as the first man was brought to the ground, I held my breath. He held his hand up, and the ringmaster blew his whistle. When the fallen man was unmasked, I saw I'd been right. He wasn't either of them. After being helped up by the ringmaster, he walked off, leaving the masked winner in the arena

Two more men came in, and once again, they began to fight. One of these I recognized. When the whistle had been blown, one of them jumped forward, thrusting mercilessly. I knew in my heart this was Caspian. His opponent was quick to raise his hand.

Two men down, and both Caspian and Milo were still in the game.

Caspian took his place next to the victor of the first

round. Another two were brought out to fight. Both of them were useless, running around each other rather than attacking, so their round went on much longer than the two rounds before. There was no way either of them was Milo. Half an hour later, the crowd began to get restless, and the two men had barely touched swords. The booing started, spurring one into action. He thrust his sword forward, piercing the chainmail of the arm of his opponent. When he saw the blood seeping off his sword, he put his hand up in submission. The guy who was bleeding won the round by default. Once the first man had been unmasked, the second fell to the floor. A stretcher came to carry him off, and the ringmaster declared him out of the competition too. Which left four more men to come. I gripped the edge of my seat as the next two men walked on.

"Milo!" I whispered. I knew in my heart it was him. I recognized his sword.

His fight terrified me more than any other, but that was because it was him. His opponent was better than the last two, but in the end, he was no match for Milo. He raised his hand.

"We have only one more round to go before lunch," the ringmaster announced. "And I've just been informed that our opponent with the wound will make a full recovery. He's up at the castle getting stitches. He's said he wants to continue the competition, so he will be back this afternoon."

Some of the crowd booed. His fight had been boring, but he was up against different men now, and there was no way it was going to be dull.

The last two came on and fought well. They were also evenly matched, but they gave a much better performance than the two who barely hit each other. I watched them closely, noting their weaknesses and where Milo would be able to beat them. Eventually, one gave up, putting his hand up in the air.

When the fifth man was unmasked, the ringmaster turned to the audience.

"Ladies and gentlemen. I'm sure you are all enjoying the show, but we are giving everyone a break. The king has thoughtfully provided food for everyone outside the arena. we'll have half an hour break and be back for the thrilling conclusion!"

"Oh, ay?" Remy asked as we all trooped downstairs to where the food was being served.

"I'm fine, Remy," I said, giving him a hug. "I just wish I'd not started this competition. I only did it to get out of marrying Caspian."

"Ca-pia!" Remy grinned, holding out a pretend sword and waving his hand around.

"Has Caspian been teaching you sword fighting?" I asked. Remy nodded enthusiastically.

Maybe I'd misjudged Caspian. I'd seen him once play-sword-fighting with Remy, but I'd thought it was for the benefit of my mother. I hadn't realized that he'd kept it up since mother was asleep.

"I'm glad he's been nice to you, Remy. I still don't want to marry him, though."

Remy seemed to understand, well, as much as Remy could understand anything. Still, he was the only one who'd picked up on my frayed nerves.

I grabbed a sandwich and a cup of juice from the massive spread. The kitchen staff had outdone themselves with the massive spread. Even with help from an outside catering company, I don't know how they managed to fix so much food. I barely had time to take a bite before we were all told to head back into the stands.

I munched down on my sandwich in a very un-princess

like manner as I took my seat and the ringmaster and the five competitors walked back in.

"Ladies and Gentlemen, Your Majesty and Your Highnesses," the ringmaster began, "welcome back to the final round in the princess competition. This afternoon will work a little differently to this morning. Now, we are going to have the remaining men fighting together. On my whistle, they will fight. The last one standing or to not raise his hand will win the hand of our princess. Good luck, everyone." He blew his whistle, and the men drew their swords. My eyes were only on Milo. I didn't care about any of the others. I watched as he started off strong, jumping right into the middle of the other four. Then everything was a blur. I knew Caspian was good, but the other three were strong competitors too. Two of them fought each other as the third, a very tall gentleman, thrust his sword at the pair of them. I turned my eyes back to Milo, watching him like a hawk as he fought Caspian, then one of the others. It seemed none of them was going to go down quickly. I'd underestimated how good the competition could be. One of the men eventually went down, brought down I thought by Caspian. He raised his hand, and the fighting was paused long enough to pull his helmet off and for him to walk out of the arena.

I kept my eyes on Milo as he once again fought Caspian. It was hard not to stand up and publicly root for Milo, but I was a princess and supposed to be impartial, despite that I'd spent the night with one of the contestants.

They were magnificent together, and although I couldn't shout for Milo, it didn't stop Charlotte screaming her lungs out for Caspian. She didn't want him to win. That would mean marriage to me, but she was caught up in the excitement of the moment, and I guess she didn't want him getting hurt. Neither did I if I was going to be honest. I'd kind of gotten used to his special brand of smugness, and though it wasn't to my taste, I didn't want to see him leave on a stretcher.

Milo was just that bit better than Caspian. I was practically bouncing in my seat as they fought. It was thrilling, and the crowd was eating it up. As Milo went for the final strike that would bring Caspian to his knees, one of the other competitors ran forward and barrelled Milo to the floor. Caspian turned to the fourth man, the tall one, as the one who'd pushed Milo down rained blow after blow down on him. The clang of metal upon metal thundered through my ears.

"Put your hand up, Milo!" I screamed. So much for being impartial. But my voice was lost in the noise of the crowd.

"Stop it!" I begged my father, but there was nothing he could do. Unless Milo raised his hand, he was still in the competition, and while he was still in, the competition would go on. The man stomped down upon Milo's leg and continued to kick and hit him. Without thinking, I stood up and raced out of the stand. If no one else was going to stop this, then I would. I raced past Hollis and down to the bottom of the stand. I knew where the men got ready. They had a separate tent. There was no one there to stop me.

I pulled on one of the suits of armor and a helmet quickly and selected one of the swords. I'd have preferred my own sword, but beggars couldn't be choosers, and I didn't have the time to run back to my room and pick it up.

The crowd roared as I raced onto the arena floor. No one could possibly know it was me, but they would know a new competitor had walked onto the field. Caspian was busy with the fourth competitor, so I raced to Milo. His armor was dented with the force of the blows from the other man. Blood blossomed on the weak spots in his armor, the places where chainmail covered the joints.

Anger surged through me as I charged the man, knocking

him away from Milo. He soon got over his shock and began to thrust his own sword. I ducked quickly as he swung his sword at me, missing me by inches. The crowd gasped as I thrust again, catching the metal of his breastplate. The sound of the ringmaster rang through my ears as he began narrating the action.

"Ladies and gentlemen, we have a new fighter. I don't even know who it is, but they are good. They are amazing. Look at these two go."

I tried blocking him out as I concentrated on my opponent, matching his speed and skill. His sword caught my arm, sending reverberations through the suit of armor, but I wasn't going to go down that easily. I thrust back as the ringmaster spoke again.

"And we have one more out of the competition."

In my peripheral vision, I saw two men with stretchers come for Milo. His hand was raised in submission. He was out of the competition.

Seeing him lifted onto the stretcher only caused my anger to intensify. There was no way I was going to marry some lout who cheated by kicking and stomping on his opponent. I thrust forward, and he began to topple. When he hit the ground, I held my sword to an exposed piece of flesh of his neck.

He raised his hand, and the crowd went wild. The whistle blew, and the ringmaster came running over. The man's helmet was pulled off. I didn't know the man, but I recognized him as one of the men fighting over the eighth egg on the mountain the day before. Looking around, I saw that Caspian had defeated his foe too. Caspian's sword was still sticking out of his chest. It had pierced right through the metal. The ringmaster ran over as I pulled my helmet off. It was over. Caspian was the winner. the crowd went insane as I bounded over to Milo's stretcher that was still on the field.

"Oh my goodness," the ringmaster said, losing his shit entirely. "Ladies and gentlemen, the fighter was the princess herself. I've never seen anything like this before!"

I ignored everything else he said and the thundering noise of the crowd as I spoke to Milo. I held his hand.

"I'm sorry," I said.

"I'm not," he replied, his face white as a sheet. "I would do this a hundred times for you. I only wish I could have won."

"It doesn't matter," I whispered back to him, tears falling down my face." I only care that you are ok."

"I think he's got a broken leg, at the very least," one of the men with the stretcher informed me. "We need to get him urgent medical care."

I nodded. A broken leg sucked, but it was survivable. Behind me, I barely registered the ringmaster announcing that Caspian's opponent was dead. What I couldn't miss was the wail from Caspian. The men with the stretcher began the walk back to the castle as I turned to Caspian. His face was a picture of utter misery. All around me, the crowd went silent, and a thrill of fear passed through me.

Almost in slow motion, I looked down to Caspian's opponent. Looking sightlessly up to the sky was my baby brother. I screamed as I remembered the ringmaster's words. Remy had sacrificed his life for me.

# 28TH JANUARY

"I didn't know it was him," Caspian cried, cradling Remy's head. Tears streamed down his face, falling into Remy's hair.

My first thought was how weird Caspian seemed without the smug expression he usually wore.

Somewhere behind me, a bell rang twelve. It was already midnight, but time stood still.

I was vaguely aware of the ringmaster telling everyone that the competition was over, and the results would be posted in the Draconian Sentinel tomorrow, but it was already tomorrow, so did he mean today or the day after?

None of my thoughts turned to Remy. They couldn't, because if what I was looking at was real, if I put any thought into it at all, then that would mean he was dead. Really dead, and he couldn't be. Not my beautiful, sweet, innocent brother.

As the world came crashing down around me, and all I could see was the anguish on Caspian's face, another voice permeated the fog.

"Why was he out here?" My father rushed over to Remy, beating the medics who were half a second behind him.

"He was out here for me." The last thing I'd said to him was that I didn't want to marry Caspian. Somehow Remy had decided to wade in and fight for me knowing that if he won, I wouldn't have to get married at all. He was dead because of me.

The crowd filed out of the stadium in silence as the medics removed Remy's armor and pulled the sword from his chest. They didn't need to confirm his death again. It was obvious to everyone that he wasn't coming back from his injury.

Caspian moved back to let my father in. I'd never seen him like this before, so raw, so utterly desolate. I don't know what hurt more. The fact that I'd never see Remy again or that Caspian was blaming himself.

"It wasn't your fault," I whispered, walking over to him, taking his hand in mine.

He didn't speak, but he didn't need to. I could see it in his eyes. He'd killed Remy, and this would kill him. He wrapped his arms around me and broke down completely, sobbing into my shoulder.

I closed my eyes and held him like that, our bodies trembling together. We were no longer enemies. We were just two people united in grief.

I wasn't aware of anything else going on around me. All I could feel was the weight of Caspian and the pain tearing my heart to shreds. Time fractured and splintered, and what felt like an eternity lasted probably no more than five or six minutes.

"Caspian!"

Caspian pulled back. I turned to see an ashen Charlotte looking at us.

"Guards were stopping people rushing out to the arena," she explained. "I had to tell them I was with you."

"I didn't know it was him," Caspian said again, this time for Charlotte's benefit. His voice was monotone and flat as though he was almost in a trance.

"I know you didn't, but that's not the point. Use magic on him before it's too late."

She grabbed his hand and pulled him away from me.

"Get out of the way," she commanded. She sounded so strong that even my father took a step back from Remy's body.

"I don't know what you mean," Caspian said. "He's dead. I killed him."

"No. You've healed people. I've seen you do it. Heal him."

Caspian shook his head. "He's dead, Char."

Charlotte almost pushed him to his knees. She wasn't the timid little thing I'd taken her for. I guess watching death changed everyone.

"Heal him!" she commanded again, pointing to my brother's body.

She ripped open Remy's tunic, exposing the wound.

Blood had already started to congeal around it, turning from bright red to deep brown. My stomach heaved at the sight of it.

Caspian put his hands on Remy's chest and closed his eyes. I'd seen him do this before when the dragons had attacked. I'd seen with my own eyes him close wounds and heal with magic.

"Can he bring him back to life with magic?" I asked, hardly daring to hope.

"No," snapped Caspian, but I could already feel the buzz of energy around him.

"I've seen it done once. Not by a fae, but by a mage," Charlotte said. "The man had only just died, and they caught him before his soul departed his body. It has to be quick before the brain completely stops functioning, but it's been less than ten minutes."

"I can't do it, Char!" Caspian hissed.

I placed my hand on his shoulder. "Remy wanted to be like you," I said to him. "He loved practicing with a pretend sword because you showed him how."

It wasn't quite the truth. Remy had often played at sword fighting before Caspian came along, but if it would make Caspian persevere, I'd say anything.

The energy around me thickened, and the weird buzzing that came along with it intensified to the point that it hurt my ears. None of the others seemed to be affected by it, but I could see that Caspian was struggling. His eyes were scrunched up in concentration, and heat radiated from him.

I took my eyes away from him for a second to see that Ash and Hollis had joined us on the field. Apart from the two medics, everyone else had gone. Milo had been taken to the castle for his own medical treatment. I'd not even said goodbye to him.

Charlotte rubbed Caspian's back as he worked his magic, but it was clear that the wound wasn't healing. How could it? Remy was dead.

"I ...can't...do..it!" Caspian said, sweat cascading from his brow.

"You can!" Charlotte encouraged, but no amount of encouragement was going to help him. He was weakening. The massive amount of energy he'd generated was beginning to wane.

I looked up. I'd never believed in gods, and even after my talks with Charlotte about the subject, I still wasn't sure I did, but I was willing to pray to anyone who would listen if it brought my Remy back. In the sky, something flashed overhead. It was no god. It was one of the dragons flying high up on the mountain. I'd seen its silhouette as it flew across the moon.

"The dragons!" My magic only worked when they were around. I could summon them, but I could also do other things when they were near. I'd splattered Caspian with magical paint right before they first came down from the sky. I held my hands up and pulled my own magical energy to me. A shot of pink light flew up into the sky. A beacon guiding the dragons. Almost instantly, the sky filled with dragons, circling down around the light, and as they did, the energy I'd felt before came back, and this time, it was magnified. It surged through me, filling me with power. As the dragons came into land around us, I placed my hand on Remy's chest. Caspian's magic merged with mine until it was one, surging through our bodies. The air around us blazed with pink and yellow light. As the last dragon landed, there was a massive flash, and then everything went dark. Only the torches that lit the arena for the benefit of the crowd remained.

"Wha...what just happened?" Ash stammered.

My body shook with both the cold and the effort, plus the remnants of the magic.

"Aza?"

"Remy!" I squealed. His chest had healed, and all that remained was the dried blood and a bruise where the sword had sliced through him. "Are you okay?" I pulled him into a hug, tears drenching his shoulder.

"Unsqua, Aza!"

I started to laugh through the enormous relief of having my brother back, and the shudders of sobs turned into tremors of joy.

"Remy win?"

He'd just been brought back from the dead, and all he

cared about was that he'd won the tournament. I didn't have the heart to tell him the truth. That Caspian had won.

"Yes, Remy. You won. You are a hero." He beamed up at us, unaware of the reason we all had tears in our eyes.

The two medics rushed to pull him onto a stretcher, but my father had to tell them to take a step back when it became apparent we were scaring Remy. Instead, he walked with us back to the palace with my father's arm around his waist and me on the other side, holding his hand.

My father took him to his bed to let him sleep, and once they were both in Remy's room, I slipped into my own, glad that the day had finally come to a close.

Later after a long bath, I threw myself into bed and slept for what felt like hours. The magic had drained all my energy from me, rendering me exhausted. I slept the dreamless sleep of the dead.

Dahlia woke me early the next morning.

"Breakfast is being served," she said, folding the clothes I'd thrown in a pile on my floor the night before. "It's just after midday, but everyone else slept in too. It's been an exhausting couple of days, hasn't it?"

"Have you seen Remy? Is he ok?"

"Okay?" Dahlia laughed." He refused to wait for everyone to get up and has already eaten breakfast. He's now waiting for everyone else to get their lazy asses out of bed so he can have a second breakfast."

I smiled. That sounded like the Remy I knew and loved. I pulled myself out of bed and grabbed some jeans and a t-shirt out of my drawers before Dahlia could wrestle me into another dress. I'd be wearing a white dress in less than a week, whether I liked it or not, so I was going to wear what I wanted up until that point.

"What about Milo?" My mind had been so consumed with Remy that I'd put Milo to the back of my mind.

"You'll see," she said. "Now get up before Remy comes looking for you. He's been harping on about more bacon for the last half hour. I swear that lad eats like a horse."

Remy grinned at me when I entered the dining room. Apart from him, the other chairs were empty.

"I expect the others will be along shortly," Dahlia said. "I'll go and see what's keeping them."

I wanted to hug Remy again, but he wouldn't understand why there were tears in my eyes, and I didn't want to frighten him. He looked pointedly at one of the wait staff who ran off and returned a minute later with a huge plate full of bacon. While I waited for the others, I pulled the papers toward me. As expected, Remy's 'death' was on the front cover of all of them, eclipsing Caspian's win. I wondered how he'd react to playing second fiddle to the man he'd branded an idiot when they'd first met. I suspected he'd be okay with it. I'd seen a side to him I'd not seen before. I'd seen love. Real love. Without realizing it, Remy had become a brother to him. I pulled the first paper toward me. I'd have to get the admin team calling the papers as soon as possible to put the record straight on Remy's death. The only paper where Remy had been relegated to the second page was the Atlantice Conch. Problems in their own kingdom trumped ours, it seemed. With a sigh, I threw the papers back down. I waited impatiently for my father and brothers to come down. Now that I knew Remy was okay, I needed to see Milo. I missed him so much it hurt, and with my wedding less than a week away, our time left together had dwindled to almost nothing. Once the papers had been set straight about Remy not dying, they would run a feature on Caspian. He would be catapulted to the most famous person in the kingdom for a brief spell, even eclipsing my mother. Thoughts of my mother were interrupted by the arrival of Ash, Hollis, and my father, who all took a seat. Just behind them came Caspian, looking like he'd just rolled out of bed and Charlotte right behind him.

"Congratulations, my friend," My father said. "Welcome to the family!"

I stood up quickly before my father had time to say anything else. Luckily, the staff had just started bringing the breakfast out, so I was able to take Caspian's hand and whisk him out of the room.

"I wanted to thank you for saving Remy yesterday," I began.

"It was me that put him in that position," he reminded me. "I honestly didn't know it was him. I would never..."

I held my hand up to his lips. "I know. I know you would never have hurt him if you'd have known."

He nodded, relief flooding his eyes.

"I know I've made it clear that I don't want to marry you, but I want you to know I'll be honored to be your wife..." I hesitated a moment, knowing what I was about to tell him. If I was going to be Caspian's wife, he had to know everything. I couldn't start my marriage built on lies. "I should be honest and tell you I slept with Milo the other night."

He nodded again, but he didn't seem at all surprised by my confession.

"Actually, there was something I wanted to tell you too."

Just then Charlotte poked her head around the door. "Are you two alright? You need to get in quickly before Remy eats all the bacon. There's hardly any left."

On her left-hand ring finger, I noticed a ring inlaid with amethyst.

I turned back to Caspian and mouthed, "Charlotte?"

He nodded again, and I swear his cheeks turned a cherry red. "Why you sly old dog!" I said, grinning from ear to ear.

He was engaged to Charlotte. I didn't have to marry him. I could now marry the man in second place. The man who had never come second in my own heart. Technically, Milo had come third, but there was no way I was going to marry the man who had stomped down on Milo. Hopefully, after the excitement of the final round, no one would notice or care.

I couldn't wait to tell him. I kissed Caspian's cheek and began the run to the hospital wing.

Milo was sitting up in bed reading a paper when I walked in. His face lit up when he saw me.

I kissed him and sat by his side on the bed. "How are you?"

"I'm fine. I heard what happened to Remy. Is he ok?"

I grinned. "If you can call eating a huge pile of bacon okay, then I'd say he's doing fine. Listen, I have an important question."

Milo arched an eyebrow as I got to my knee at the side of his bed.

"I know it's customary for the man to ask the woman, but it's also customary for a princess not to compete in a tournament to win her own hand in marriage, and since when have I listened to customs and traditions anyway? Milo...will you marry me."

He pulled me into a kiss that said it all, except it didn't.

"No," he replied in a whisper. "I want to marry you more than I've wanted anything my whole life. I would do anything for you, and that is why I'm saying no. I want you to go to Urbis and do what you have to do. I want you to go with Nyre and save your mother. I want the wedding you talked about a couple of weeks ago where your mother cries tears of joy as you walk down the aisle. Come back to me when you are truly ready for marriage and ask me again. I'll wait for as long as you need."

"But...I'll wait, and you can come with me to Urbis."

He shook his head. "I'm not part of your adventure. My

leg will take six weeks to heal, and I don't think you'll be able to wait that long. I'll still be here. Then we'll have our own adventures. I've changed my mind about going to The Forge. My mother will have to visit us here." He kissed me again, and this time, I fell into him. Nothing else mattered.

We were interrupted mere moments later by my mother's maid calling for Dr. Augusto to come quickly. My mother was getting worse.

I ran to get my father from the dining room. He was busy tucking into his breakfast and reading the Atlantice Conch.

"Atlantice is having some dreadful times," he mused as I ran in. "It's almost as if the darkness is spreading there too."

The darkness. In all the excitement over the past week, I'd forgotten that dark magic was coming back into the kingdom. Derillen was still out there somewhere, and we were no closer to finding her.

"Father..." I wheezed. "It's Mother... Dr. Augusto wants to speak to you."

"The queen's health is fading fast," Augusto said as we all crowded around my mother's bed five minutes later. My father and my brothers had all dropped their breakfast to follow me to my mother's room. "A curse it may be, but her body cannot sustain it much longer."

My father lowered his head into his hands at Augusto's words. I could feel his pain as acutely as my own. This was breaking him.

"How long does she have?" I asked through streaming tears.

Augusto shrugged. "I cannot say. A month. Maybe two."

Having just gotten over Remy dying and then being brought back to life, my heart wasn't ready for the loss of my mother too.

"Maybe Caspian can bring her out of this," I babbled. "He saved Remy from death."

"No," Caspian said. He'd been so quiet coming into the room that I'd not noticed him. "This is not like Remy. Remy's brain waves were still there. Your mother isn't sick, and she isn't dead. You know the only way to bring her back. Either find Derillen or find Morpheus."

"Derillen?" My father asked. "Not this again!"

"Alec, my dear friend. I think it's time we faced the truth. She is back. Azia is sure of it, and so am I. Charlotte thinks Briar Rose is trapped in Morpheus's dream world. We've invited Azia to stay with us in Urbis while she looks for him."

I noted the use of the word we. It seemed Caspian's time here was finally coming to a close. And more surprisingly, he was going home with Charlotte.

A thought struck me. I ran from the room and up to my own. From under my bed, I pulled out a box. A box that held a magic necklace. I ran back with it and handed it to Caspian.

"Charlotte thinks this is a necklace from the gods. Will this save her?"

Caspian took the necklace from the box. I'd not thought to show it to him before now.

"This is very powerful. I've never seen anything like it." The stones changed from diamonds to amethysts in his hands. I'd never seen anything like it either. "Where did you get this?"

"It doesn't matter. Will it help her?"

Caspian laid it carefully around her neck, clasping it at the back.

Color came back to her cheeks, but she didn't stir.

"This is miraculous," Dr. Augusto said, feeling her pulse. He performed a couple of checks, but after a minute or two, his excitement waned. "I think you've bought some time with this necklace, but she is still cursed."

"Father," I began.

Without speaking, he stood up and walked over to me. Taking my hand, he pulled me outside of the room.

"I know what you are going to say to me. I've known this was coming for days. After the courage you showed at the competition, I have no reason to stop you now."

"So, you mean..."

He nodded his head.

"I know when I have been wrong, and it seems I have been wrong about a lot of things lately. I've made mistake after mistake, and you've tried telling me over and over again. I'm sorry for everything I've done to you."

I brought him into a soggy hug.

"You didn't do anything, Father. Are you really allowing me to go to Urbis?"

"I think I've learned enough to know that you'll go with or without my permission, but you have it if that makes it easier for you. My permission and my blessing."

"Thank you."

"I'm counting on you, Azia. I can't let her die."

I nodded my head. "She won't. I have Nyre to take me there and Charlotte and Caspian to help me find Morpheus. I have everything I need."

"You cannot travel by dragon," My father replied. "It is a nice idea, but you'll be spotted way before you get to Urbis. I don't want anyone knowing you are there."

I furrowed my brow with frustration. "Then how? If I take the Urbis Express, people will surely recognize me."

"Take one of the castle horses. I think I owe you one for your birthday anyway, and you won't have to count on a tiny dragon hauling you all the way there. You can still take your friend. She's one feisty girl, and I rather like the idea of you being looked after...even if you can fend for yourself."

I grinned. "That would be great. Thank you, Father."

"Since we have time, I think we should go eat first. It's not every day I send my daughter out into the world by herself."

"Not by myself. I'll be going with Nyre, remember, and Charlotte promised to let me stay with her and Caspian in Urbis."

"You know. I always thought you were too good for that chap," he said, draping his arm over my shoulder. "I'm rather glad he's engaged to that Urbis girl."

I shoved my father playfully in the side.

Later, I stood in the castle entranceway, waiting for my family to come and wave goodbye to me. My bag was packed, and I'd picked a horse for the journey, a black one aptly named Adventure. The kitchen had outdone themselves with so much food it would last me for days.

The morning papers were out on a side table. I sorted through them until I found the Atlantice Conch. Something about their story intrigued me.

Eventually, everyone came out to wish me goodbye. Father, Remy, Ash, and Hollis, as well as Caspian hand in hand with Charlotte. Dahlia shuffled out behind them, and lastly, on crutches, Milo joined us.

We all walked out into the courtyard where Adventure was waiting.

Nyre flew around up in the air waiting for me to leave.

"I still can't get over my big sister kicking ass!" Ash explained, thrusting an imaginary sword at Hollis the way Remy liked to do.

I felt for the dragon sword by my side. I'd not been able to use it in the tournament, but I knew it would keep me safe on my adventure. I'd never be without it again.

"I know, right?" agreed Hollis. "You should make her a knight, Dad."

"She's better than any knight!" My father replied, pulling

me into a hug. "You stay safe in Urbis. I want my daughter home in one piece!"

I took a deep breath. "Actually, I'm not going to Urbis."

Everyone looked at me with surprise. I'd been thinking about changing my plan for the last day or so. I only had Charlotte's word that Morpheus would be there, and even then, she wasn't so sure. He was a slippery character who only left the house of the gods when it suited him. No, I had more of a chance looking for Derillen. I was sure she'd left Draconis. None of my father's men had found her. But something was happening in Atlantice. Something awfully familiar. Whatever had shifted in the magical energy here, it seemed had happened there too.

"I'm going to Atlantice."

"Atlantice?" my father asked. "Whatever for?"

"I will go to Urbis," I explained, "but I know in my heart that whatever is happening in Draconis is spreading and think it's going to hit Atlantice first. I've been seeing strange news reports in the Atlantice Conch for a while, but it was only this morning that I put two and two together."

"Please keep in contact," my father said. "Send letters when you can so we know where you are. I know the Royals in Atlantice. Be sure to seek them out. They will help you."

"I will," I said, kissing his cheek. I'd already said goodbye to my mother, but this was somehow harder. My father was aware of how dangerous my journey could be.

I hugged Dahlia and my brothers before getting to Caspian. There was so much I wanted to say to him, but nothing would come to mind. I was sure I'd come up with a million things once I left. "I'm glad I didn't kill you," I said.

He grinned. "And I'm glad I didn't kill you." He brought me into a hug, and for the first time since we'd met, we came together as friends.

Then there was only one person left to say goodbye to,

and this was going to be the hardest goodbye of all. I'd kept it together so far, but tears were already beginning to form as I took Milo's hand in mine. The others walked back to give Milo and me some space.

"I'm going to miss you," I said, my voice cracking with emotion. "You are the best fake, almost fiancé I ever had."

He snorted a laugh. "And you were the best princess I almost got to marry."

"Princess, you will marry someday!" I corrected him. He brought me into a kiss. Our last...for now.

Afterward, I jumped up on Adventure. He brayed a little when Nyre came to rest on my shoulder.

Tears streamed down my face as the horse began the first part of our journey. A journey that would take me first to Atlantice and then who knew where. I wanted to think that I'd find out what I needed in Atlantice, but something deep within me knew we'd end up eventually in Urbis. That was where my story had begun. That was where my story would come to an end...

Carry on the adventure in Atlantice with The Little Mermaid in Queen of Mermaids

# A NOTE FROM THE AUTHOR

The Kingdom of Fairytales authors hope you enjoyed this new way of reading. We don't think that a series has ever been set with one chapter a day thought a whole year before and we hope we did it justice.

With this in mind, please leave a review, but when you do, remember that these books were always meant to be short breaks in your day and the blurb reflects that.

We would LOVE it if you can drop us a few words on Amazon

Review here

## AFTER THE HAPPILY EVER AFTER...

There is more to these stories. You want to know what happens next right? Fast forward eighteen years…

Pick up book one now

PREQUEL

SLEEPING BEAUTY

1. Queen of Dragons
2. Heiress of Embers
3. Throne of Fury
4. Goddess of Flames

LITTLE MERMAID

5. Queen of Mermaids
6. Heiress of the Sea
7. Throne of Change
8. Goddess of Water

RED RIDING HOOD

9. King of Wolves

10. Heir of the Curse
11. Throne of Night
12. God of Shifters

RAPUNZEL

13. King of Devotion
14. Heir of Thorns
15. Throne of Enchantment
16. God of Loyalty

RUMPELSTILTSKIN

17. Queen of Unicorns
18. Heiress of Gold
19. Throne of Sacrifice
20. Goddess of Loss

BEAUTY AND THE BEAST

21. King of Beasts
22. Heir of Beauty
23. Throne of Betrayal
24. God of Illusion

ALADDIN

25. Queen of the Sun
26. Heiress of Shadows
27. Throne of the Phoenix
28. Goddess of Fire

CINDERELLA

29. Queen of Song
30. Heiress of Melody
31. Throne of Symphony
32. Goddess of Harmony

ALICE IN WONDERLAND

33. Queen of Clockwork
34. Heiress of Delusion
35. Throne of Cards
36. Goddess of Hearts

WIZARD OF OZ

37. King of Traitors
38. Heir of Fugitives
39. Throne of Emeralds
40. God of Storms

SNOW WHITE

41. Queen of Reflections
42. Heiress of Mirrors
43. Throne of Wands
44. Goddess of Magic

PETER PAN

45. Queen of Skies
46. Heiress of Stars
47. Throne of Feathers
48. Goddess of Air

URBIS

49. Kingdom of Royalty
50. Kingdom of Power
51. Kingdom of Fairytales
52. Kingdom of Ever After

# JOIN US

Would you like FREE Kingdom of Fairytales Coloring pages? Click the link below to pick your free gift up.

Kingdom of Fairytales FREE gift

Check the Kingdom of Fairytales website for competitions, news and info on all the books and authors

Kingdom of Fairytales Website

Or Join us on our Kingdom of Fairytales Facebook page for fun, games and author takeovers

Still want more? Completely immerse yourself in the Kingdom of Fairytales experience and pick up exclusive offers and gifts

Become a Patron

# THE KINGDOM OF FAIRYTALES TEAM

These books would not be written without a great many people. Here is our team:

Many thanks to those who have made this possible.

Thank you to Rhi Parkes without whom, this series would never have come about.

Thanks to all the authors.

J.A. Armitage, Audrey Rich, B. Kristen Mcmichael, Emma Savant, Jennifer Ellision, Scarlett Kol, R. Castro, Margo Ryerkerk, Zara Quentin, Laura Greenwood and Anne Stryker

Also thank you to our amazing Beta team

Nadine Peterse-Vrijhof, Diane Major, Kalli Bunch and Stephanie Pittser.

Thanks to our Proof Reader

Tina Merritt

Thank you to our Patrons

Gigi Nickerson, Amanda Hurst & Coralee Butterfield

## ABOUT J.A.ARMITAGE

J.A lives in a total fantasy world (because reality is boring right?) When she's not writing all the crazy fun in her head, she can be found eating cake, designing pretty pictures and hanging upside down from the tallest climbing frame in the local playground while her children look on in embarrassment. She's travelled the world working as everything from a banana picker in Australia to a Pantomime clown, has climbed to the top of Mount Kilimanjaro and the bottom of the Grand Canyon and once gave birth to a surrogate baby for a friend of hers.

She spends way too much time gossiping on facebook and if you want to be part of her Reading Army, where you'll get lots of freebies, exclusive sneak peeks and super secret sales, join up here

https://www.subscribepage.com/v7o8k4

Somehow she finds time to write.

Printed in Great Britain
by Amazon

60696957R00076